Take the Stairs

Take the Stairs

by

Karen Krossing

Second Story Press

NATIONAL LIBRARY OF CANADA CATALOGUING IN PUBLICATION DATA

Krossing, Karen, 1965-
Take the stairs / Karen Krossing.

ISBN 1-896764-76-2

I. Title.

PS8571.R776T34 2003 jC813'.6 C2003-905167-6

First published in the USA in 2004

Edited by Kathryn Cole
Cover art by Marilyn Mets
Text design by Lancaster Reid Creative

Printed and bound in Canada

Second Story Press gratefully acknowledges the support of the Ontario Arts Council and the Canada Council for the Arts for our publishing program. We acknowledge the financial support of the Government of Canada through the Book Publishing Industry Development Program, and the Government of Ontario through the Ontario Media Development Corporation's Ontario Book Initiative.

Published by
SECOND STORY PRESS
720 Bathurst Street, Suite 301
Toronto, Ontario, Canada
M5S 2R4

www.secondstorypress.on.ca

To Mom, Dad, and Barb

For the many obstacles
we have overcome
together

Contents

The Building

SIXTY-FOUR WILNUT STREET. A fifteen-storey brick building butted against a pocket of comfortable houses. One face of the Building looks lazily across four lanes of traffic to a shabby strip mall. The other face ignores its tired playground to gaze at the houses nestled on the lip of the valley. Round green trees hide the valley floor. But back to the Building.

Balconies are crammed with bikes, empty beer cases, and broken furniture. A shopping cart stands deserted outside the front door. The super, Mag Jennings, slouches and smokes in the lobby. The halls hang heavy with the smell of roach spray and the rivalry of tonight's meals. And behind the tightly locked apartment doors: the drone of a television, angry voices, and a troubled sigh.

Dusk settles over the Building. Blinds lower; curtains snap shut. The Building closes to the few people still lurking outside and tightens around the secret hopes of those within. The Building.

Hide and Seek 

Apt. 312

I STOOD APART AS THEY CALLED out the rules to the game, a hint of roach spray from the Building still clinging to me.

"Tony's it." Jennifer smiled at him. Her skin white and her hair dyed as black as a bottle of ink.

"The signpost is home free," said David, breaking out of the sullen mood he'd been in since his dad had died.

"No going inside." Flynn's voice echoed off the Building.

The Building was officially called The Monteray, although anyone who lived there just called it the Building. It was like any other run-down building in any other city. No one stayed long, if they could help it.

"Why is Tony it? I want to be it." Louis was the youngest at fifteen, although we were all too old to be playing hide and seek.

The crickets halted their thrum as I walked across the grass toward the others. Twilight on a summer's evening. Day giving over to night. The sky turning a menacing shade of indigo like a deep, violent bruise.

"Tony's it," Flynn yelled. Louis looked like he wanted to run him over with his mountain bike. "Got to stay within the compound. No going in the underground. Everything else goes. No home free. No time out. Once you're caught, you join the search. We play until everyone's found. How many of us are there? Twelve? OK. You've got to find eleven, Tony."

Flynn talked as if only he knew how to play, but he was lousy at hiding.

Then Flynn saw me. "Hey! How about a game of hide and seek, Petra? You in?"

I nodded.

"OK! You've got to find twelve, Tony!"

"Petra's too hard to find," Roger said. He was a lumbering, gentle Black guy who was always easy to catch.

"I can find her." Tony shoved him playfully. "Let's start the hunt."

I said nothing.

"Look who's talking, Rog." Magda draped a tanned arm around my shoulder and smiled with white teeth at Roger. "Weren't you the one who went up to your apartment to watch TV last time? Came down after your show was over." Giggles and jeers.

I almost smiled. Magda—polished golden hair and topaz eyes. With my black hair and olive skin, we looked like complete opposites. Yet she was the only person that I could maybe talk to. That I might be able to trust.

"That's it," said Flynn. "Petra plays. Ready?"

Nods and muttering all around.

Then Flynn saw Asim heading to the Building. "Hey, Asim! The game's on."

Asim was walking, tall and silent, beside his short, round mother in her headscarf. He called to Flynn. "I can't. I have to baby-sit."

"Later then." Flynn turned with a jerk. "Let's go. Tony, count to 30."

"I'll give you 20," said Tony.

Flynn opened his mouth to argue, but Tony began to count. "1, 2, 3, ..."

I turned toward the Building and crept along the shadow of the wall, my body compact. I'd worn my hair in a long braid, and black clothes for camouflage. Flexible fabric for running, and something I could sleep in, just in case.

Everyone scattered—through the playground, around the pool, among the huge garbage bins, under the trees. Cori led Allie behind a bush to hide. Tanya joined them too, even though there wasn't enough room. She was dressed in army boots and a bright tie-dyed dress that could never be hidden. Together they laughed and squirmed, as if they hoped to get caught.

I shook my head. Maybe they didn't see the danger all around. Maybe they didn't need to practice. Passing them, I moved through the grounds with my eyes shut. A test of skill. I crept across the grass, not opening my eyes until I sensed I was right before a tree. Bull's eye! I scrambled up the dark side. My first hiding spot would be high above the ground where I could watch.

I had known that I was different from the others for a while—that they couldn't see in the dark. That I had a heightened instinct for survival. I learned it from my mother's cat.

Smoke, she called it. It was gray with glacier-blue eyes. Not a friendly cat, although it did blend well with the evening shadows in our apartment. When the room filled with the scent of violence—sweat and blood, fear and hatred—it found a tiny space where it wouldn't be seen. I watched the cat move under the low coffee table, behind the couch, around the floor lamp. Its motion was so fluid that it never got hurt. Not like my mother. He smacked at her with big fists. Tossed her easily across the room. My mother, soft and fleshy, like a bruised peach. Her hair was black clouds. Her sounds soft moans, raspy breaths, whispered secrets to herself in Mandarin. Given the choice, I followed the cat.

From my hiding spot, I watched Tony find Jennifer without effort. Jennifer had hidden under the slide where Tony could see her. She had a thing for him, although it wouldn't last long. It never did with Jennifer. Jennifer sprinted away from him in her tight black skirt and he bolted after her, grabbing her around the waist. To catch her, he just had to touch her, but he tackled her to the ground.

Laughing, Jennifer and Tony rolled around together. Then Jennifer pushed him off and brushed the grass and candy wrappers out of her hair. Just as they began to search hand-in-hand, Flynn peeked around the corner of the Building.

"Get him." Jennifer pushed Tony after Flynn.

As Tony tagged him, Flynn said, "I was home free. I was touching the pole."

He pointed to the signpost, which was nowhere near him. No Ball Playing.

"Yeah, right," said Tony. "You said there was no home free."

Jennifer caught up to them and stood beside Tony.

"Oh, no! I said the pole was home free. Right, Jennifer?" Flynn turned beggar's eyes on Jennifer, his desire for her on his face.

Jennifer shook her head and rubbed against Tony's arm.

"I tell you, I was touching that pole."

"Listen, turd. No way you were touching that pole," said Tony, hands on hips. Jennifer giggled.

"Takes one to know one," muttered Flynn.

Tony made a fist in front of Flynn's face. He would have walloped Flynn except that Roger wandered out of hiding.

"Tired of it already?" Jennifer laughed.

"Yeah, well. I've got to go." Roger yawned. "There's a good movie on soon."

They all laughed at Roger as he lumbered toward the Building, scratching under his arm with slow, thorough fingers.

"What a couch potato," said Flynn, the fight forgotten.

Then Allie, Cori, and Tanya started whispering. Their hiding place was near my tree, but I wasn't worried. If anyone did look up and see me, they would still have to tag me.

Tony, Jennifer, and Flynn heard them too, and the chase was on. Tony caught Allie easily because she froze in panic. Flynn tagged Tanya because her dress tangled her up. Cori was a problem—she tried to climb my tree. Using stillness as my shield, I willed myself to melt into the branches. Jennifer pulled Cori down, scraping her arms against the rough bark.

"Hey, watch it!"

Jennifer ignored Cori and squinted up into the tree, but darkness wouldn't give me up.

Then Sidney broke from her hiding place behind the cluster of boulders beyond the playground. Sidney was small but fast. She ran through the parking lot and out of sight. Running for her life. Running far away from us all. The others gathered themselves up and ran after her. Only then did I move.

I slipped down the tree to find a new hiding spot, because the secret to not being found is to keep moving. I padded over to the unlit pool, slid through the half-open gate, and lowered myself into the water without a ripple, my fingers over the edge. The water still held the warmth of the sun. No one would look for me here. Not even my father.

I never looked at my father anymore, although his furious white face was a warning flag in my mind. Skin contorted by cracks of anger. Blue eyes blazing hate. Look at him and be turned to stone. The stone of death, or worse, the stone of living death like my mother. I knew his bitter stench after a night at the tavern. His heavy breathing as he stalked his prey. The smack when he caught my mother, then the animal cry from her throat.

He grew more powerful as he beat her. I could see the rush he got from it, but she couldn't feed him enough. He began to need strength from new sources. He turned to me.

Thinking of him, I was surprised to hear his voice. Then I saw his silhouette framed by the light from the side door. The door shut with a hollow clang and darkness consumed him until he stepped under the lamppost.

"Where is she? Where's my kid?" he called out in a rumbling voice, clenching his fists.

"I wish I knew," Tony said.

A few others laughed. I was sure they wouldn't give me away. Not that they could ever find me.

A scowl crossed my father's face, then he almost brightened. "You're playing hide and seek? Tell you what. Just to make the game interesting, I'll give twenty bucks to whoever finds Petra and brings her up to the apartment." He peeled a bill off a wad of cash and flashed it around. Then he added with fake concern, "She's late. Past her curfew."

"I don't know." Magda was with the others.

"What's the big deal?" Cori asked. She always thought about herself first.

"Yeah!" Tony said. "I could use twenty bucks!"

"We could share it with Petra," suggested Magda.

"We'll do it, sir," said Flynn. Echoes from the others.

That stopped the game, or gave it a sinister new twist. Everyone began to search for me. My father lurched back into the Building.

I pushed down the panic with a gulp and coiled into a tense spring, waiting for a chance to get clear of this mess. Memories of what my father could do flooded me, and I fought not to lose my concentration. He'd only caught me once, but that was enough. He'd banged my head with one fist, then the other, and he'd thrown my body around the room. But I wasn't in my body. I'd hidden from him, left my body behind. I was a rock, strong and everlasting. Now, he had returned for me, even used Magda against me. The game never ended. How long could I hide?

"Here she is," came a shout, too close. "Help me."

Footsteps on the concrete. The squeak of the gate pushed open. Four hands lifted me dripping from the pool. How was I found? Thinking about my father was my weakness. My distraction. I had to focus.

"Let's take her in."

I hung still in their arms, as if dead. Waterlogged, my clothes were clinging, my braid dripped down my back, and goosebumps prickled my skin. I needed time to think. Tony. Jennifer. Cori. Flynn. He had changed them—cast his blood-red gloom over them. Did everyone have claws? Was no one safe?

I had to protect myself. I could trust no one. My heart pumped faster and blood flowed into my muscles, preparing for the fight. Then I became the jungle cat I was. I snarled with claws extended, searing flesh from bone. Scratching eyes. Kicking shins. Until I was free. Until the hands released their grip.

I ran to the driveway and straight down the ramp to the underground. Glancing back, I saw only a track of wet footprints slowly fading as my sandals dried. The garage door was just scraping shut after a car. I rolled under it then ran again, my wet clothes now caked with dirt. Blinked in the fluorescent light. The scent of stale oil and gas stung my nostrils. I veered into the back seat of an abandoned car where I sometimes slept.

Forcing my breathing to slow, I wrung the water out of my braid and brushed most of the dirt off myself. Then I curled, soggy and shivering, into the old blanket that I had brought once, and ran my fingers along its satin edge for comfort.

Would they follow me? I would have to stay alert and not give in to sleep. I had too much to lose. The future that stretched out before me. The promise of escape. My life. No one would take that away from me.

Then I thought, why hide? Maybe I should seek. Seek a way out. Seek a place without him. My mother might choose to stay, but I wouldn't.

An engine started up. An old blue pick-up. I dropped out of the car and sneaked down the row until I was near the ramp, hidden in the shadow of a post. The yellow-green ceiling lights buzzed indifferently. Like the Building couldn't care less what happened to me.

I listened for the others. Watched. Nothing. The pick-up edged out of its spot and toward the garage door. The wheels rolled over the trigger cable and the door began to creak open. A man sat idle in the driver's seat, waiting for the door to lift. Windows shut. Crooning Frank Sinatra music loud enough for me to hear.

The door opened fully. Brake lights dimmed.

I dashed for the truck. Swung into the back and squatted down as it pulled up the ramp and heaved over the potholes. I peeked into the cab at the driver, my heart hammering. If he was aware of me, he didn't show it.

The driver turned past the garbage bins. I saw Louis and Allie heading in for the night. Where were the others? Had they given up looking for me? Maybe. Tony and Flynn were still out. Magda, Jennifer, and Cori.

I wanted to stand up and shout to them—to come out of hiding—but the risk of losing my ride was too great. Instead, just as we neared them, I dared to stick my head up over the edge. Waved one arm in triumph. Waved goodbye to the Building.

Jennifer saw me first. Cori yelled and pointed. Tony and Flynn with surprised eyes, mouths dropped open. Beautiful, golden Magda smiled. Waved me off like a queen.

If only Mom were with me. I crouched back down and tried not to think about her, alone with him. Maybe I could come back for her.

The truck's engine rumbled through me as we rattled and bounced away from the Building. Rows of darkened stores with only a few dim lights breezed past us. I shuddered in my wet clothes. Where would I go? A shelter? My grandmother's place, west of the city? I didn't know yet.

There is a time to hide and a time to seek. I had mastered hiding. Now, I had to learn to seek.

Tailwind

Louis

Apt. 1517

I THREW ONE LEG OVER MY MOUNTAIN BIKE and powered up the pedals. I'd just finished a can of pop—my traditional swallow of rocket fuel before take-off. My stomach was pleasantly bubbling with a delicious mix of gas, sugar, and caffeine. I'd slept late then gulped back a breakfast of eggs and toast. My bike buzzed beneath me. We were ready for the Path.

I discovered the Path last year. Had to have some way of getting around. I wanted to share Dad's car with my sister Gina when I turn sixteen next month, but Dad said, "Your sister needs the car to be safe in the city, Louis." I never got why she was so special.

The Path, just two blocks from the Building, was a web of bike trails that ran through the city valleys. There were the regular asphalt paths as well as a few dirt trails that a lot of city bikers knew about, with some small hills and a few jumps along them. Yet for me, the Path was the rugged tracks that the gang carved out of the valley hillsides. From hard-packed clay to sand so fine it was just dust. Steeps that were near impossible after a rain. Fallen tree trunks, thick shrubs, and natural rock jumps that could kill.

I was on my way to meet the gang for a ten o'clock. It wasn't too hot for July, so I decided to go for a ride first. Try a few technicals and practice my skill. I was still trying to master Drop Dead Curve.

The drop into the valley was a long slope on a track of tar. I pumped the brakes only a little—the Path was dry and clean—and leaned back as the cool valley air rushed over me. Then I noticed it was more crowded today. Very crowded.

There were the usual people. Some retired wrinklebags out for their daily airing and a yummy mummy with long brown legs pushing her kid in a stroller. Of course, Bob was in his usual spot on the bench, shaking his arms and talking to himself. Bob wasn't his real name; we just called him that. He was one of the homeless guys who built cardboard shacks up on the hillsides.

Yet something was different about the Path today. Droves of novices were everywhere, riding cheap bikes that they had probably bought the night before. Then a couple of hammerheads raced past me down the hill, one on either side.

"Get out of the way," one of them shouted, an evil smirk on his face.

I could tell they were both corporates who worked in the big office towers downtown. Corps, we called them—dead to the real world. Full bike suits, stuffed panniers, cell phones, and top-of-the-line bikes without a scratch on them. I wouldn't mind gear like that, but I wouldn't become a corp for it.

I started to get smoked up inside, but I tried to let it go. I challenged myself. Speed up and show them how to do it.

I pushed into action, caught up, and even passed them, but I was grunting with the effort—couldn't get my engine going. My first ride of the day and I had the lung capacity of a newborn squirrel. Pathetic. They blew by me as if I were parked.

"Told you to get out of the way," smirking guy said with a laugh.

"Idiots," I muttered, but I wondered what they were doing out so late in the morning.

I turned off onto a single-track. Actually, it was only a half-track. One of our private trails. I wouldn't want to meet another biker because there was no room to pass. A vegetable tunnel—just tree trunks on either side and leaves that smacked against me as I passed. It was a shortcut through the trees that met up with Drop Dead Curve. I'd give the curve one try then head over to the Rock.

I burst out of the trees and onto the wider trail, but I didn't expect to see the two corps that had passed me earlier, travelling with me toward the curve. What were they doing on our track?

I nearly got sideswiped by one of them. He yelled something at me that I didn't hear, because my heart was in my ears pounding out a new drumbeat. I caught a movement of his foot out of the corner of my eye. Was he trying to kick me out of the way?

Then Drop Dead Curve was on all three of us, and I wasn't ready. We were too close together, the smirking guy out front and me level with the kicking man. I was going too fast. I couldn't take the run wide enough with the guy on the outside. I leaned into the corner but my bike started to skid. I dabbed at the ground to catch my balance, but it was no use because of the fist-sized rocks that multiplied daily on the curve.

Kicking man pushed ahead of me, which was good because I was about to part company with my bike. A warning thought flashed into my brain. Get off the bike in a hurry! My upper body twisted in a last-second attempt to save myself. I bailed off my bike and then I was falling, my hands out to meet the gravel like I could push the ground away from me. My arms buckled, and I did a graceless face plant into the trail.

I heard the prang of my bike as it crashed, smelled the dry dust in my nose, and tasted dirt. Stars of pain swarmed around my head but I lurched up in a hurry. Quick enough to watch the corps flying down the trail. A nearby chipmunk scolded me. A jay sang a victory song for the corps. They could make Drop Dead Curve.

I wished for a bike like theirs so much it hurt. Maybe then I could make the curve. Why did everyone else always have better gear?

I looked for my bike. We'd both managed to avoid the trees. I took off my helmet and shook my brains back into place, dusted the gravel off my hands and knees, examined the fresh rip in my T-shirt, and checked out the damage to my bike.

I had gotten my bike at a police auction for next to nothing. It had a few nicks and scratches on it to begin with, but I'd added plenty of my own. Each scratch told a story—when I'd flipped over the handlebars and smashed into a tree, or when I'd slipped on a pipe and bent the wheel like a taco. It wasn't much of a bike compared to some, but I guess we were OK together.

Not much damage. A few new scratches, but I could still get around. I got back on and spun the pedals slowly over to the Rock.

* * *

THE ROCK WAS A FLAT GRAY BOULDER halfway up the east side where we hung sometimes. It was mostly hidden by trees and had a great view. There was a natural burrow under one side where you could cool off in the shade.

The whole gang was there, scarfing down some snacks that someone had brought. Probably Silver, whose real name was Juan. He had managed to get a part-time job at a bike store so he sometimes sprang for a bag of chips. I had gone for that job too, but they didn't want me. Too young, they'd said.

Other than me, the valley gang was Silver, a tiny Mexican who was the fastest pedaller in the city; Three-speed, Silver's tag-along little brother; Jumpster, the only girl and a quick learn for any new tricks; and Cyclops.

Cyclops was the only one who wouldn't wear a helmet. He had a thick bony skull, considering the number of times that he'd landed on his head on solid rock and lived to torment us further. I was sure that his brain was full of tiny air bubbles, just like an Aero bar. It had to be, after all those smashes. He had earned his name from a huge purple wound he once got on his forehead. His eyes had been swollen shut, and the open wound looked like a huge, bloody eye.

Cyclops saw the scratches on my hands and face. “Dropped on the curve again, Newbie?” His lips were dusted orange from the chips.

On the Path we didn’t use our real names. They called me Newbie because I hadn’t earned my name yet. Only a great feat got you a great name.

I grabbed my water bottle for a drink, wishing that my helmet could hide my face. I hated being called Newbie, but if I told Cyclops, then he’d just say it even more.

“I could do Drop Dead Curve a year ago,” said Three-speed.

Why did Silver let him come along?

“Yeah, yeah.” I squirted water over my face. “What’s going on with the Path today?”

“Don’t you know?” Jumpster was pushing with her arms against a tree trunk, stretching out the back of her legs. I couldn’t help but notice her form, and my internal temperature rose 12 degrees. “Transit workers went on strike at midnight last night. The corps took over the Path this morning. It’s an invasion.”

“Whoa! I met two guys who tried to run me down, but I didn’t know anything about this.” I tried not to show that I was watching her. I was sure she’d never be interested in me.

“Madmen with helmets.” Silver shook his head. He believed in fair play, but the corps didn’t.

“Wait until this afternoon.” Jumpster shielded her eyes from the sun and scanned the valley paths that were spread out before us. No one said anything because we all knew that Jumpster was right. There was always too much traffic after any workday. This afternoon would be insane.

* * *

WE HUNG IN THE VALLEY for the rest of the day, but the morning migration and the strike were all we could talk about. No new tricks or trails that day.

By 4:30 the corporate take-over was in full swing. We retreated from the tar tracks and watched from a break in the trees on one of our private paths. One rookie, outfitted in the latest gear, was walking his bike down the hill. Probably afraid of wrecking it. Others were pushing by him, swerving and cutting each other off. We watched several near misses at the blind corner by the river. More than once there was almost a stack of mutilated bikers.

"The strike should give them an excuse to stay home," said Silver.

"No." Cyclops made a stupid-looking face. "All they think is 'Gotta get to work. Gotta get to work.'"

Yeah, I thought, as simple-minded as Cyclops. Yet I didn't dare say it or he'd bop me one.

Then two bikers were screaming down the track toward us at top speed.

"It's them!" I screeched and pointed at the bikers. "The guys who ran me down this morning!"

Kicking man and smirking guy were raiding our private paths again. I was furious and Cyclops was raging, too.

"We carved these tracks," he yelled at them, as he straddled his bike in the middle of the trail.

They just raced through the trees around us. Cyclops spit and snarled after them, then he chased them. He was in such a bad headspace that we all followed, but it turned out that the corps were in a worse place. Because when they saw Cyclops tracking them and screaming threats, they got crazy, too. Just as Cyclops got up even with them, kicking man grabbed a dead tree branch while he was on the move and threw it at Cyclops' wheels. I couldn't believe it. Cyclops was down—an involuntary dismount into the dirt. The branch lay between his twisted spokes.

"Are you OK?" asked Silver as he helped Cyclops disentangle from the wreckage.

Cyclops was rubbing his head—he must have hit it bad. He was a little cross-eyed, and I bet the world was blurry to him.

"Urban survival, man," he said. "We gotta do something."

For once we all agreed with Cyclops, but no one knew what we could do about it.

"We can't keep people out of the valley," Jumpster said.

"We could sabotage the Path." Cyclops' mouth was twisted into an ugly grin and his eyes were burning. The fire spread through me too, like a disease.

"Naw, too dangerous," said Silver. "We don't want to get anyone killed."

"Yeah." I stifled a laugh. "But we could change the paths that we made, couldn't we? Like Drop Dead Curve? Maybe it needs a jump."

I was joking, but I wished we could do it. Then the sky started to darken with serious storm clouds. The tea party broke up, and we all headed for home.

* * *

I ONLY HAD TO TRAVEL ON A MAIN STREET for three blocks on the way home, but I could see the fallout from the strike. The streets were mashed full of cars—one person in each—as they fought their way home. One driver skimmed too close to me. I rode behind the tailpipe of an old Honda and choked in exhaust. By the time I got to my turn-off, I was glad to get away.

As I rode toward the Building, I got a knot in my stomach. The Monteray, visitors called it because of the cracked white letters on the sign out front. Must have been named after some stuffy rich duke or a greasy business tycoon. Wherever the name came from, the Building was a useless hole overlooking where the highway exit-ramps sliced the green of the valley into pieces. The hallways reeked like twenty different dinners stirred together in a pot and left to fester. When the elevator broke, which was at least once a week, I had to carry my bike up fifteen flights of stairs or leave it outside to get stolen.

Dad said we had to stay because the rent was low. I tried to shrug it off, and I avoided people from the Building when I could. Especially after that game of hide-and-seek last month when Petra disappeared. Not that I had anything to do with it, because I cut out early. Cori told me that Petra had been kidnapped. Someone else said her father was a beater. You never knew what would happen at the Building, but everyone was always ready to gossip about it.

Stopping near the back door, I planned to do a little maintenance before the storm hit. A quick trip up to the apartment for an old rag and I was giving my bike a scrub-down. My sister pulled in—just returning from her shift at the hospital cafeteria in Dad's junker Mercedes, which was almost as old as I was. I squirted my bike chain with WD-40 to try to clear the sand and didn't give Gina much of a look. She was circling the upper parking lot, searching for a spot. She hated the underground.

Gina turned the car left just as she passed me and yelled out, "Clean mine next, Bike Boy."

Anger flared inside me. I had to buy my bike while she got to use Dad's car. Just because she found a job and I didn't. Not that I'd ever give up my bike—I couldn't bear to. Yet I sure wouldn't mind a little equal treatment. Gina was always talking about how unfairly women were treated, but I only saw how she got all the favors and I got nothing.

I scowled at my sister. She laughed. Her hair was pulled back under an ugly hairnet. I was going to throw my greasy rag through the window at her stupid face, but before I could, something on the car came loose. A flash of silver clattered down and bounced toward me. It stopped just a step away.

I reached over to pick the thing up. It was the hood ornament off the front of Dad's car. Maybe it was a message. My sister hadn't noticed, so my prize became a sneaky reward for something. Enduring Gina, I guessed.

It was light. I tossed and caught it with one hand. Wouldn't add much weight. I would strap it onto the front of my bike. A Mercedes hood ornament. Maybe it would bring me victory over the curve.

A brutal thunderstorm raged all evening, but at least it was happening at night. I wanted to see the valley in storm, but I couldn't from my bedroom window. So I went to the bathroom and stood on the edge of the tub. The window was high up on the wall and the bottom half was frosted. I could see the wind shaking the trees and lightning threatening to set the valley on fire. Thick, steamy mud would clog the trails tomorrow, but I didn't care. Nothing would stop me from cruising the Path.

* * *

THE NEXT DAY, YESTERDAY'S WOUNDS had turned into ribbons of cooked bacon on my hands and cheek. My skin felt tight and I was a little sore, but I had to try Drop Dead Curve one more time.

My sister was mad because Dad said she had to share the car with him for the rest of the strike. He'd walked to work the first day, but it had taken too long. I was glad that Gina had to get up early to drive Dad. The morning without her in the apartment was excellent. I blasted *my* radio station and walked around naked after my shower. Then I set out for the Path with my new good-luck charm taped to my handlebars.

By the time I got there, the valley was overrun more than yesterday. I noticed more garbage than usual, and I was ticked off that they were trashing the Path.

I headed across the vegetable tunnel to Drop Dead Curve for my usual practice crash. Before I hit the curve, I saw Cyclops and Jumpster roosting on the side of the trail. They signaled me over. I wanted to get to the curve, but I could stop for Jumpster.

"Got yourself a Mercedes." Cyclops fingered my dad's hood ornament.

I was about to tell him how I got it, but Jumpster waved toward the curve. "Cyclops did it. He built that jump you were talking about."

"What jump?"

Just then Silver showed up with his little brother, and Jumpster gave us the scoop.

Cyclops had dragged several logs across the track, piled them just before the curve, rooted them into the earth on either side, and built a ramp up. Only Cyclops could have done it by himself—he had arms thick with muscle. He walked us all through it, and we talked about how to take the jump and the curve.

Cyclops looked at me and said, "Hit the brakes after the jump and you'll be in pieces."

"Treacherous," said Silver.

"No problem," squeaked Three-speed. His voice cracked sometimes.

I rubbed my hands together and was reminded of the sting of yesterday's wounds. My whole body tensed up. More pain. I couldn't even do the curve without the jump.

How could I ever do it with the jump?

Jumpster didn't say anything. I was sure she wasn't worried about handling it. She was the best jumper of us all.

"Bet those corps can't make it." Cyclops said. "Too much lycra and titanium. Not enough skill."

We waited around all morning for the corps. Parked our bikes in the woods and huddled close to the curve to watch, which was a drag, because I wanted to be out riding. Because a pack of ants wouldn't leave my ankles alone. Because kicking man and smirking guy were no-shows. So what was the point?

"They bagged out on us," Cyclops said finally, his teeth pressed tight together and his neck muscles bulging.

"Maybe you scared them off." I just wanted to get back to riding. I had some moves to practice.

Just as I was about to suggest we give up the watch, we heard someone coming down the trail.

"Get down," Cyclops hissed. We all ducked behind the bushes.

Then kicking man and smirking guy appeared. Like some kind of cheap TV movie where the bad guys always show up on cue. And they were heading straight for Drop Dead Curve.

After hours of being forced to wait, I didn't care much about the corps anymore. They were the lowest form of animal, but I wasn't out for revenge like Cyclops. I didn't care if they could do the curve or not. I just wanted to know if I could.

Without saying a word, I left the gang and scuttled in a low crouch back to my bike. They didn't notice—all eyes were on the corps. As I yanked my bike vertical and made my way through the scrub, I could see the corps through the trees.

I witnessed it all, but I was distant, out of touch, disconnected. I could only feel my bike under me and my blood pumping with a wild energy. My brain was filtering out everything else. I watched half-blind as the corps swerved in crazy loops before the jump. They had seen it and were trying to avoid it. They both skidded sideways into the dirt. Gravity check. I heard Cyclops howl out a war cry as he charged out of the bushes at them.

I pushed my bike out of the forest and onto the trail. I rode back up the trail and did a 180. The corps were walking their bikes around the curve fast and hightailing it back down to the tar track. Cyclops was spewing and swearing after them, and Three-speed was hopping up and down beside him.

"First blood on the curve!" yelled Cyclops in triumph. He whopped Three-speed on the back and knocked him over.

The gang noticed me then, ready to do the jump. I saw their faces, surprised. Silver ducked his head and moved off the track. The others followed.

"You'll be hamburger, Newbie," Cyclops called.

I ignored him and started my ride before I got too scared to try.

I sighted the best line over the jump and around the curve. Yet before I even got to the jump my body stiffened up and the bike travelled a bit away from me. Then I was on the ramp, nervous and jittery, and I told myself to see it through. No turning back now.

My bike took off into the sky and there was nothing but air under me. I stopped myself from squeezing the brakes to get control—if I landed with my front tire locked I'd crash for sure. Then my front wheel hit the ground spinning and jetted me toward Drop Dead Curve.

I wavered a little too close to the edge of the trail and pruned the bush with my helmet. My head spun and I fought the urge to plant my heels into the ground. Then I was hydroplaning across a mud puddle that the rainstorm had left behind. Fast enough that not too much goop got in my brakes and gears. I got through the puddle without plowing to a stop, and with a little more confidence. I had made the jump and I wasn't down yet.

I had a sudden, unexpected burst of energy. Where it came from I didn't know, but suddenly I was stoked. I twisted like fire toward the curve.

I remembered to slow down for the corner. I stayed on the upside of the trail and made a wide arch, looking only at the inside of the curve where I wanted to go next. With my weight on my outside pedal, I leaned hard into the corner until I almost fell to the inside.

My front wheel made it over the loose rocks on the curve then I started accelerating again and in no time I had negotiated Drop Dead Curve clean. No crashes. I couldn't quite believe I had done it. I pulled to a stop further down the trail and looked back to make sure.

"I did it!" I yelled, shaking my fists at the sky and letting out a whoop of joy.

In Dad's car, my sister could beat me in a race any day, but I could make Drop Dead Curve. With the jump. On my beautiful old bike. It was incredible. I felt like I could ride up a vertical rock face with no problem. I was glad for the transit strike. I was glad for kicking man and smirking guy. Because everything had come together for this moment.

Then Jumpster was running down the trail. On foot. She skidded to a stop in front of me and looked at me curiously. What was she thinking?

"You were in the zone, weren't you," she said, so close I got a whiff of her flowery shampoo mixed with the salty scent of summer sweat.

I was a little shaken, caught off-guard. I had never had the courage to look right at her. Her eyes were a gorgeous warm swirl of green and golden-brown. Her face was flushed from the heat, and a damp lick of hair swung down one side of her face.

"I don't know." I'd heard them talk about the zone before, but I'd never been sure what they meant. I couldn't tell if I had been in the zone or not, but I was loving the attention of Jumpster.

Her wet, pink lips opened into a smile, and she didn't take her eyes off me. Even when Cyclops hustled up behind her and broke the moment. Sometimes, I could kill him.

"Maybe you just had a good tailwind," she said as Silver and Three-speed showed. I noticed how none of them tried the curve.

"Tailwind." Cyclops took up the word and tried it out. He slapped me hard on the back. I struggled not to fall over. "Guess you earned your name, Tailwind."

I was speechless. I broke a grin. Maybe I did have an invisible force behind me, directing me. A tailwind.

I sneaked another look at Jumpster.

"I couldn't have a better name," I said to Cyclops, even though I couldn't care less about him. Jumpster was still smiling at me.

Grains of Sand

Apt. 220

"PASSIONLESS PACKAGES OF PORK MEAT." That's what Mark called his parents, and most adults. Mark said that *we* would experience *all* of life. The joy and the sorrow. The love and the suffering. Not just feeble feelings, but violent emotions that would erase our power to think. Passions that would take complete possession of us.

Mark wanted to become a writer. He wanted to move people with his words. He wanted to go to university for English after our world trip in the summer. He had his life planned out, and mine.

I headed down the stairs to Mark's room in his parents' basement—where we had spent many passionate afternoons instead of going to science lab. The familiar smell of damp gym socks, musty books, and scented candles calmed me. Dusty sunrays streamed light through the two small windows. I could breathe deeper in this room, which was wider and longer than my whole apartment.

Across the room, Mark was bent over his huge wooden desk, staring down at something he'd written, willing characters into life with the power of his pen. He didn't look up. Was he writing me another poem?

My toes dug into the deep carpet as I tiptoed around his waterbed toward him. He was a little too skinny with a narrow face, a pointed nose, and a thin mustache. Yet his hair was black silk under my fingers, and his blue eyes sparkled when he got excited about what he loved—writing poetry and me.

I kissed the back of his neck and buried my nose in his sweet-smelling hair. Then I just said it, trying to still the quiver in my voice.

"Don't you wish we could keep the baby?"

"Just a minute. I'm thinking."

His words were a knife, cutting through my hopes.

I held my breath and waited, marvelling at the artist before me even though I was hurting. On his desk was *The Metamorphosis* by Franz Kafka. Mark had read it three times, and I'd read it, too. Mark liked me to read the same books he did so we could talk about them. This book was about a man who woke up one day to discover that he had changed into a giant bug. Overnight, he had become a disgrace, an outsider, an alien. I could relate. I woke up to discover a baby growing in my belly.

"Huh?" Mark finally looked up.

I said it again, with less hope this time. "Don't you wish we could keep the baby?"

His faced looked pained. He let out a sigh. "We've talked about this already, Magda. We decided this together. A baby doesn't fit with our plans. And we've already made the appointment."

I wasn't really asking to change the appointment. I knew I was too young to have enough money, food, and even love for a baby. Only seventeen. I was able to have a baby, but not able to raise one. Something didn't seem right about that. Still, Mom had dropped out of high school to raise me. But I didn't want her life. I didn't want to live in the Building forever. It was too confining, too limiting. At the Building I was only the mistake my mother had made when she was fifteen.

"Hey, Sidekick?" Mark tried to tease away the dark clouds that were gathering around us. He didn't like the usual love names—sweetie, honey, snuggle-bunny. He said they didn't mean anything because everybody used them too much.

Mark didn't get it. When I asked him if he wished that we could keep the baby, he was supposed to say yes. Then we would hold each other and cry together about how we couldn't. About how we were kept in chains. How we had the bodies of adults, but were only given the responsibilities of children. And how we were blamed for messing everything up.

Yet he didn't get it.

"We can't keep it, Magda. You know why we can't do that."

A lump grew in my throat.

"He's not an it." I could feel the baby was a boy.

"You know what I mean." He tried to hug me but I stiffened and pulled away. Mark shrugged and turned back to his writing. I saw the hurt look on his face and was glad.

I knew all the reasons why we couldn't keep our son. We had talked and talked and talked about it. Yet Mark was supposed to pretend. He was supposed to understand that I needed to mourn with him. Mourn the loss of our child.

Petra would have tried to help, but she'd vanished in the summer. If only she were here. But then, I guess I wasn't there for her.

If I told Mom, she would understand how I wanted to make something with Mark, but she would never listen to talk of keeping the baby. According to her, I was supposed to make different choices than she had. Lead the life that she couldn't.

Only Mark could understand how a baby would be so nice—someone for him and me to love. Someone we could hold onto forever.

* * *

I KEPT THE APPOINTMENT. Mark came, too. The hospital was an ancient, brown brick building with several modern sections awkwardly built on. I travelled down the dingy hall, flat on my back in a crinkly blue robe. Mark jogged beside me, holding my hand in his limp grip. I was afraid they would wheel me past mothers admiring their new babies behind smooth glass, but we saw no mothers, no babies.

The nurse dropped Mark off at a crowded waiting room. Mark ducked his head and hurried in. He had his writing pad and his favorite mechanical pencil ready. I tried to say goodbye, but the words got caught in my throat.

Thankfully, I was sedated—calmed into a false sleep. A sleep that could obliterate the harsh truth, for a short time, anyway. For only in a drugged state could I allow the unspeakable to happen. Allow those few living cells to be pulled from my body.

I woke later to a stabbing pain in my gut and the warmth of blood between my legs. The room was spinning, expanding and contracting. I shivered under a thin blanket and inhaled a smell like floor polish. I tried to lift my head off the pillow, but a lead weight had replaced my brain. "Mark?"

A nurse came instead.

"Just rest. Shh. You're at the hospital." A mask covered her mouth but her eyes were friendly.

Then I remembered why I was there. The baby was gone. I shut my eyes to force the tears back. I wanted no pain. No feeling. Anesthetic.

"Don't come back to me again," the doctor said at my six-week check-up. "Abortions are not birth control. Take precautions. I will not help you again."

As if I hadn't taken precautions. As if the condom had never broken and my pills were one hundred percent effective. As if I had planned for it to happen.

* * *

I WAS NUMB FOR A LONG TIME AFTER THAT—afraid to feel, unable to cry. Even after my body had healed, I couldn't touch Mark, and Mark didn't try to touch me. Maybe he didn't want me anymore.

Graduation came and went. Mom gave me a present. A donation toward my 'round-the-world trip with Mark. I had been saving for a year, working at the grocery checkout.

Now I had enough to go. To leave my life behind and find a new one.

The morning of our trip, Mark and I sat in his sunny basement room with our gear spread between us, each sewing a Canadian flag onto a backpack. Today, we would load our backpacks with our sorrows and our dreams. Today, we would take off in a plane. Today, I figured, was the day our baby should have been born. Alexander. I had named him Alexander.

He had Mark's black hair and my round face. I could catch glimpses of him playing on the floor between Mark and me as we packed. Gurgling happily. A line of drool sliding down his chin. Shining innocence and rainbow love at me with big pancake eyes.

He was my imaginary child. I had let him slip away, but he was happier where he was. Because he would never hear the slap of anger. He would never feel the cool breeze of Mark's selfishness. He would never know my betrayal. He would grow up with love, play in green parks with budding trees, and eat sugary snacks in the sticky-sweet sunshine. He would be safe in his motherless, fatherless world.

I finally wept. Tears that flowed a river of sorrow from my body. My baby was dead but not forgotten.

Mark watched my tears, but he didn't hold me. I wanted him to cry, too—find some way to celebrate death and rebirth.

"Come on, Sidekick," he said finally. "Are you homesick already? Don't worry. It's just jitters. You'll be better on the plane." He pulled a paper from his back pocket. "Here, this will cheer you up." He read his latest poem—his thin mouth pumping words at me like bullets.

Lovers,
Like grains of sand,
Rolling and bumping against each other,
Groping,
To quell the aloneness
Of human clay
With sensual illusions
But never,
Never finding the life-love of touch.

"Mark, you do understand! We've been divided since the baby. So alone. But now ..."

"Baby?" His astonished eyes showed that he had managed to forget. Then the shadow of a memory passed across his face. A spasm, then it was gone. "Oh, that. I thought we were finished with that." A pause as he wiped his mind clean of the mess. "Powerful poem, isn't it?" Mark beamed at me with a sunny smile, his blue eyes glinting.

I cried more tears. Not because of Mark's poem. Not because I would never feel Alexander's touch. Because I saw that Mark—with all his talk of passion—was choosing not to feel. Not to feel the loss of Alexander. Not to feel the torment I felt.

"Glad you like it." He folded the paper and put it back in his pocket, still smiling. Then he pushed the backpacks, clothes, and other gear aside. He wiped my tears, wrapped me in his insubstantial arms, and kissed me.

His lips were thin and dry. Kneeling on the scratchy carpet, I remembered hours of delicious nonstop kisses, never getting enough. I remembered when we discovered the broken condom—how I had joked that he'd be buying diapers soon. I could afford to laugh then, because I couldn't get pregnant on the pill. I wasn't making the same mistakes my mother had. I guess the joke was on me.

Mark kissed my neck and ran his hands through my hair. His lips pressed mine against my teeth. His fingers were prodding and he smelled sour. Yet I refused to pull away. Mark may choose not to feel, but I never would. I squeezed my fingers into the flesh of his shoulders and cried harder.

* * *

AT THE AIRPORT WITH MARK. We were burdened with backpacks, airplane tickets, and a fistful of traveller's checks. Mark's parents had dropped us off, waved goodbye to us as we entered the boarding area, and aimed their Volvo for home. We checked our backpacks, and Mark started to talk. I didn't. I listened.

"I can't wait to get to London," he said. "An adventure, Sidekick. An escape from mediocrity. Out to see the world—to taste all its treasures. To experience all its pleasures. To gather a writer's wisdom. And who knows—maybe publish a couple of poems along the way? Who's to say I couldn't do it? There's nothing holding me back. Nothing holding me down. I'm as free as a naked baby after a bath."

Baby? How could he talk about babies?

I scrunched my ticket in my fist. I narrowed my eyes at him. He wouldn't pretend we could keep the baby. He wouldn't feel the pain with me. He wouldn't even admit it had happened. And now he was talking about babies?

A fire raged to life within me. Mark was still talking, but I had stopped listening. I was listening to myself. I didn't want to go to England. I didn't want to go with Mark. I didn't want to be with him at all.

I started to walk away. Mark noticed his audience was gone.

"Hey, where are you going? We're about to board."

I kept walking. I'd just been a mirror in which he could admire his reflection. He could find another mirror.

"Sidekick, you'll miss the plane."

I turned. Two lazy men in suits, bored with the wait, were watching us, their ties like tongues hanging out, drooling.

"Sorry, honey-bunch-of-love. Can't go," I called across the divide between us, knowing the love name would annoy him.

Mark's weasel face showed shock and astonishment. He squinted his narrow eyes and shook his skinny head. "What?"

"I can't be your sidekick anymore."

"Magda! Don't!"

Mark lunged out of line then stopped, hesitated. The line began to surge through the doors. He looked from me to the line, panic on his face. I knew he would be frightened alone, but I wasn't sorry for him. Maybe it would make him feel.

Mark stepped back in line. Shaking from my act of courage, I turned my feet toward the door. Mark didn't call to me again. His dreams were calling to him and he was listening to them. Oceans lay between us now. We lived on different continents. Every step I took away from him carried me further along my own path—a winding, twisting journey with many choices, many directions.

I left the boarding area. I left Mark. I would cash in my ticket and get my pack back somehow. Then maybe I would find a taxi—use my traveller's checks to take me somewhere far away from the life that awaited me at the Building. Travel to a new city; find a job and an apartment. Maybe I could find Petra. Maybe I would go to college. Maybe I'd call my mom.

Opportunity

Flynn

Apt. 606

APARTMENT 601. HUNTER'S PLACE. I waited for the hall to clear. My heart ka-thumped in my throat. When the guy with the big cardboard box got on the elevator, I turned the doorknob, praying it would be locked.

It opened. Damn.

The place was dark. I hoped that Hunter would be asleep by now. There was no sound but it stunk like stale beer. Tony's words and the thought of beer pushed me through the doorway and into the kitchen. I could hardly see. I tiptoed in my sock feet, tripping over Hunter's cat on the way to the fridge.

"Yowl!"

I swallowed a scream. The cat darted under the table. One lonely plastic chair was pulled up to it. I ducked, ready for Hunter's big fist to find me—to bash me for sneaking into his place.

Silence. I breathed out slow. Where was he? Why was I doing this?

Earlier that evening, Tony and I had been hanging out in front of the Building. A Saturday night and we were dry. Nothing to do and no money to buy some fun.

Then Hunter had come slowly up the steep drive to the Building. With one arm, he was pushing a grocery cart full of beer up the hill.

"Look at that!" Tony had said.

Hunter was a giant—even taller than Tony. He could probably break me with a snap. "One, two, three, four, five." I'd counted the two-fours in the cart. "What I would do for a few of those!"

Tony had glanced sideways at me and grinned with his eyes sparkling. "Maybe there's a way. Everybody knows that Hunter doesn't lock his door."

"With arms like those he doesn't need to."

Tony had talked me into it somehow. It wasn't stealing, he'd said, it was taking advantage of an opportunity. Two hours later, here I was sneaking around Hunter's apartment.

I found Hunter asleep on the couch. He was sitting upright, not even snoring, and he reeked of beer. Old beer. Beer from nights of drinking.

Weird guy, I thought. Who sleeps sitting up?

The fridge filled the kitchen with light when I opened the door. Empty! Then I saw the cases piled beside the stove. He didn't even keep them cold? I loaded my coat pockets with bottles, trying not to clink them together. Easy work. Hunter slept on the couch the whole time. I could fit two beers into each of my deep side pockets.

Three for me and one for Tony, I thought. That was fair since he wasn't doing the dirty work, right?

Maybe I could have carried a few more with me, but I didn't want to stick around any longer. Besides, my apartment was on the same floor. No telling who I might run into on the way out.

* * *

I TOOK THE STAIRS DOWN. The side door to the Building groaned shut behind me. In the dark, I tiptoed in my sock feet over the concrete slab toward the abandoned playground. Rocks prickled my feet and the ground sent spikes of cold through my toes. An empty Doritos bag blew up in my face, trapped by a whirlwind that spun in useless circles. I slapped the bag away, skirted a puddle, and hunkered down on the bench next to Tony.

"What'd you get?" Tony slouched against the bench, one arm slung over the back. His legs hung open like slack jaws. My three-day-old Nikes were beside him. Tony had said he would hold them for me. He'd said to take them off so I could tiptoe real quiet.

"Give me my shoes." My feet were ice-cold and wet. My long brown overcoat hung loose around me. After my cousin Dan had worn it for four years the lining was patchy, but at least I looked like a slick operator in it.

With a huge grin, Tony hugged my shoes to his chest, his big shoulders curved forward like a gorilla's. We had this friendly rivalry, mostly because we both were after Jennifer, but sometimes Tony went too far.

"What'd you get?" he said again in a teasing voice.

"Give me my shoes and I'll tell you."

Tony made to throw one of my shoes into the pool.

"OK. Don't."

He grinned wider, lowered the shoes, and sat on them.

I sighed, imagining my Nikes crushed by his butt. Why did Tony get everything he wanted? First Jennifer, now my shoes. Well, he wasn't going to get any beer then. He didn't deserve it. Right?

The eyes of the Building winked at me as people snapped their lights off and yanked the curtains shut. I chose my words carefully. "Hunter was asleep. God, he's massive." That part was true. "There was none in the fridge. I looked everywhere."

"You didn't get any?"

"Well, ..." I had to think fast. I pulled my legs up under my coat and curled my fingers around my toes to warm them. I moved carefully so that the bottles in my coat pockets didn't clink together and give me away.

"You didn't?"

"Like I said he was asleep. He was on the bed and I could see some cases under the bed, but they were jammed in."

"Didn't you try to get them out?"

"No way. I tell you they were jammed. If I tried to move him ..." I shuddered, just to make the lie better. "That bed hung like a hammock."

The door to the underground creaked open. An ambulance siren sounded in the distance, coming closer.

"Maybe you should go back and have another look around."

"I'm not going back. Forget it, Tony."

"Have it your way." Tony stood, grabbed one shoe, pulled back, and let it fly.

"No!" I tried to jump for it, but it sailed over my head—a white bullet in the dark.

I punched at Tony's chest, which was level with my face. The burly stench of him so strong I could taste it. Tony pushed me off.

The shoe fell short. Inches from the edge of the pool. I eyed Tony, who grinned at me again. The best pitcher I knew. Kicked out of the Junior A's for fighting, but he could hit the nose of a dog with a spitball when he wanted to.

"God, Tony. Did you have to?"

I pulled a brown bottle out of my coat pocket.

Tony took the beer and tossed me the other shoe, still with that twisted grin on his face. "I knew you were holding out. Could smell it on you. How many did you have in there?" He twisted the cap off and began to chug it back.

I shouldn't have downed that beer in the stairwell. With a sigh, I shoved my foot into the shoe and ran lopsided for the other. As I jumped the chain-link fence around the pool, the last two bottles in my coat clanked. I swore once, then again, when I examined the long scuffmark on my other shoe. I jammed my foot in and dashed back to Tony.

"Hey, don't drink it all. I only got one," I said.

I watched Tony's Adam's apple bob up and down.

Tony stopped, burped, and wiped his mouth with the back of his hand. The bottle was empty.

"Yeah, right."

He grabbed my coat and shook until it clanked.

"All right. Let go."

I pulled the two beers out and passed one to Tony.

"Cheers." He grinned and clinked bottles with me. "To Hunter."

* * *

AFTER THE BEER THERE WAS NOTHING TO DO, so we headed in for the night. I dragged into my apartment in my long coat and scuffed shoes. Mom was asleep in the dark in her precious La-Z-Boy chair. A book of crosswords on her lap. Her jaw open to a whistle snore. Her purse beside her on the floor. Another opportunity.

I tiptoed to her purse. Red lights flashed onto the ceiling, probably from an ambulance or a cop car down in the circle. I kneeled down beside her and began to rifle through her purse. Adrenaline pumped through my veins. This was easy. I could get away with anything.

On the way to her wallet, I found a fully stocked makeup case, tweezers, cough drops, a stack of coupons clipped together, and a silky black ribbon that her grandmother had given her for some reason that I'd forgotten. Then I saw her wallet, the change purse open, and a fiver hanging out like a gift.

I reached for the five then changed my mind and put my hand on the ribbon. When I rubbed my thumb along its silky smoothness, I sank into a Jennifer fantasy. I would wrap the ribbon around her black hair and brush my hands over her powdered white neck. She would twirl around and say how Tony was just a mistake and she really wanted me. Then she would plant a long kiss on me with those painted red lips. I could feel it now. The smear of lipstick, her breath in my mouth, her eyes shut to the moment, her fingers running through my hair.

My mother snuffled, held her breath, then exhaled. One eye was half open.

I grabbed the five for myself and the ribbon for Jennifer. I knew that the ribbon was special to Mom—she'd been holding on to it ever since her grandmother had died—but I needed it more than she did. Right?

My mother opened her other eye. I acted cool.

"Whozat?" she mumbled.

"Just me, Mom." I kept my voice chipper as I stuffed the bill and the ribbon into my coat pocket.

"Flynn?"

"Come on, Mom. Time for bed." I let her slouch over my shoulder all the way to her room.

"You're such a good son." She rubbed a hand over my short hair.

"Sure I am." A thrill ran through me as I spoke. I could get away with this. Opportunities were everywhere.

I pulled back the covers for her. She tucked herself in beside Dad.

In my room, I stripped to my underwear and climbed under the covers. The red lights were still flashing, and I wondered what weird thing had happened in the Building this time. Like in the summer, when Petra had ridden away in the back of a truck, never to return. She sure took a game of hide and seek seriously. In the next room, I could hear Dad flopping over in bed then snoring again. I punched the pillow down over my ears and tried to sleep, even though my toes were still ice cubes. Tomorrow, I'd give the ribbon to Jennifer.

* * *

I COULD NEVER FIGURE OUT WHY JENNIFER didn't go for me. She'd been with a lot of different guys, so why not me? Yet with the ribbon tucked into my coat pocket that morning, I was going to win her. She and Tony were just casual. I knew I had a chance.

I went outside to see what was happening. I found Tony, David, and Tanya in our spot behind the thick pine trees, leaning against the big boulders that had been there forever. Jennifer was there too, sprawled across a larger boulder. Her black lace top clung to her breasts.

I winked at her, without Tony seeing, so she would know that I was still interested, but she turned away. No problem, I told myself. She just didn't see me. I kept my shoulders back and my chest out so she could spot the work I had been doing with the weights.

"Did you hear?" Tanya said as I sat on a rock with graffiti on it. "Hunter's dead."

Tony gave me a look that said, *talk and you're dead*, but I was too stunned to think straight.

"Hunter's dead? He can't be! He was just fine last night."

"What are you talking about?" Jennifer rolled her eyes.

"Oh, we saw him lugging in a few cases of beer last night." Tony covered for me.

I could only wonder—was I the last person to see Hunter alive?

"What happened? Was he murdered?" I asked, trying to sound casual. Inside my head I was beginning to flip out. How had Hunter died? He was fine when I was there. Or was he? He hadn't even snored. Was I going to get in trouble?

"Murdered? Flynn, you are so weird." Jennifer turned up her pointy nose at me.

Tony gave me a shut-up-about-Hunter-or-die look. His shaggy eyebrows were knotted like two duelling caterpillars.

"Didn't you hear the noise last night?" Tanya asked. "The ambulance? Three police cars?"

David began to look uncomfortable. He was skinny and small in a leather jacket that was too big for him. I guess he was thinking about his Dad, who had died just a little while ago.

I nodded my head.

"Well," Tanya began to pace excitedly, then she settled next to Jennifer, who shifted slightly on the rock to give her some room. "Apparently Hunter's door was open last night and Mag Jennings went in to check it out. She almost fainted right on the spot because there was Hunter dead on the couch! He must have had a heart attack or something. Later, everyone was down in the circle watching Hunter get loaded into the ambulance. It was a real show! Crazy Tate crawled into a police car and turned on the siren. They almost arrested him but he took off." She laughed. "Anyway, I heard one policewoman say that the cause of death was no mystery, but that they had noticed evidence of tampering. Can you imagine? They were dusting for fingerprints and everything."

I could hardly move. My jaw hung loose and my arms dangled slack at my sides. What had I done?

"What ..." I managed to say.

David interrupted. "I've got to go." He pushed his way through the pine trees, letting them scratch him up.

"Gone to cry it off." Tanya looked after David, almost forlorn.

"I say good riddance. He gives me the creeps," Tony said.

"It's not his fault that his dad got AIDS." Tanya crossed her arms and glared at Tony.

"Yeah, well, his father was a flamer and he's probably one, too." Tony snarled.

"So what if he is? What's wrong with that?" Jennifer's face was red. I'd never seen her that mad. Tanya was staring curiously at Jennifer.

Tony backed off. "Cool down, babe."

"Whatever!"

"What are the police doing now?" I said.

"I don't know." Tanya shrugged. "Looking for suspects, I guess."

Tony lit a smoke and the conversation moved on, but I didn't.

The police would be looking for me. Did I leave any fingerprints? Would they know they were mine? What would they do to me if they found out that I was in his apartment? I glanced at Tony but he was ignoring me for Jennifer, who must have made up with Tony because she was rubbing against him like a kitten. Did she have to do that in front of me?

I slid off the rock and shoved my hands deep into my coat pockets. With one hand, I felt the ribbon against my fingers. It was supposed to be Jennifer's, but she was too busy with Tony.

I scrunched the ribbon into a little ball and let it fall to the ground beside me. With my not-so-new Nikes, I squished and crushed it through the pine needles and into the brown earth.

Jennifer wasn't good enough for the ribbon.

* * *

THREE DAYS LATER, I CAME IN from an evening of watching TV with Asim. Asim had to baby-sit his sisters and brother as usual, but it was better than doing homework.

I expected Mom to ask about my homework, but instead I found all the kitchen cupboards open, her purse emptied on the table, and a trail leading off down the hall. Mom was in my room, rifling through my drawers and flinging my shirts onto my unmade bed.

"Hey! What are you doing?" I stood in the doorway and tried to sound offended, although mostly I was terrified that she would find the condoms that I had hidden so hopefully at the back of my underwear drawer.

Mom looked up at me. Her short hair was messed up like she'd been pulling at it and her eyes were wide with worry.

"Flynn." She said my name as if she were surprised to see me. Then she looked around my room, distracted.

"You're taking my room apart!" I planted myself in front of my drawers.

"I'm sorry, Flynn. I didn't mean to. I've lost my black ribbon and I just have to find it."

My heart began to rattle in my chest.

"Well, I didn't take it." I crossed my arms and frowned at her, trying not to betray my lie.

"No, of course you didn't. I've just misplaced it somewhere." She sounded sincere, but I wasn't so sure.

"So why are you going through my drawers?"

"Was I?" She rubbed a hand through her messy hair and looked at my ransacked drawers. "I guess I was. I just thought that it might have fallen in with the laundry somehow. Really, Flynn, I am sorry."

"Oh." I picked up a T-shirt and tossed it into an open drawer.

"I'll clean up," she said.

"No. I'll do it myself." I crammed two more T-shirts into the drawer.

"All right. If you see my ribbon, will you let me know?" Her forehead was wrinkled with worry lines.

"All this for that old ribbon?" I pretended not to understand, but I knew that it was important to her. Why had I taken it anyway?

She hung her head and dropped onto my bed. "I guess it does sound a little silly, but ... oh, you know the story already."

I nodded my head. When would she get out of my room?

She sighed. "I always kept it with me. Grandmam gave it to me when she died. What could have happened to it?"

Just then Dad thumped down the hall. He stuck his head in my bedroom doorway and asked, "Did you find it?"

"No." Mom sighed again, heavily.

"I'm sure you'll find it, Mom," I said, planning how I would get the ribbon back.

She squeezed me tight. "I hope so, Flynn."

The doorbell rang.

Dad answered it. When he called me, I ignored him.

"Flynn, come now!" Dad's voice was more urgent the second time.

"What? I'm busy."

"You need to come." He pronounced each letter in each word so clearly that he pulled me to attention.

I wandered down the hall, expecting maybe Tony or Asim. I never expected the police.

Two large uniforms stuffed with muscles filled the doorway.

"Flynn Sheffield?" said the cop with the red hair. "I'm Constable Jeffries and this is Constable Davidson. We want to ask you a few questions."

The huge Black cop, Constable Davidson, stared me down.

I blinked and tried to find my voice.

Dad frowned down at me. Mom put a protective hand on my shoulder.

"OK," I squeaked.

Dad stepped back and, with his back straight, invited them in. I shoved my hands into my jean pockets to stop them from shaking.

Constable Davidson had to duck his head to get through the doorframe. Sitting on the couch, side by side, the two huge cops could have broken through the floor into the apartment below. Wouldn't the old coot underneath us be surprised when they crashed down on top of him?

Dad brought in a kitchen chair and set it in the middle of the room. "Sit," he pointed at the chair. I sat.

"What is this about?" Mom asked as she perched on the arm of her La-Z-Boy chair. "Is Flynn in trouble?" Then she added, "He's a good boy, you know."

Good old Mom. I stole her money and pulverized her grandmother's ribbon and she praised my honor. Guilt swamped me. My throat was too clogged for me to speak. Yesterday I'd spent her five dollars on fries and gravy at school. Some good boy.

"Your boy is not in trouble, ma'am, as far as we know." Constable Davidson's voice rumbled through my chest. "We just want to talk to him about the death of a Mr. Hunter."

Why didn't I feel any better?

My mother's eyes widened and she gasped. "Kind old Mr. Hunter is dead?"

Hadn't she heard?

Dad, standing next to her, took her hand and patted it. I slid down lower in my hardback chair and tried to prepare for the assault.

Constable Davidson boomed out questions at me about what I had seen that Saturday night and how well I knew Hunter. Or, Alexander Hunter. I had never heard his first name. The red-haired cop, Constable Jeffries, wrote everything down in a small notebook. I didn't tell them anything that would incriminate me.

It was obvious that they only knew what Tony and the Building's gossips must have told them, which was that Hunter came back to his place at about nine o'clock with enough beer for everyone in the Building. They asked if I'd seen any suspicious characters lurking in the corridors. I said no. Constable Davidson called them "corridors," not halls. It didn't make the Building seem any grander.

Of course, Tony wouldn't have told them how he had talked me into sneaking a few bottles for us. Or how he knew that Hunter always forgot to lock his door. No, Tony would never have told them that.

The questions lasted forever. I squirmed on my chair. Mom and Dad looked from me to the cops like they were watching a tennis match.

Just when I thought they would never leave, the cops stood up. But by then I was thinking, I deserve to be arrested. I never should have taken those beers, or Mom's ribbon. I was almost ready to confess.

"One more thing," Constable Davidson turned back just as we almost had them to the door. "Mr. Hunter's daughter, Mrs. Joanna Sterling, discovered that a few items were missing from the apartment. A watch. A television set. And $5,000 cash."

Mom gasped. Dad frowned and his mouth became a stern, tight line. I tried to hold myself steady. $5,000 cash! What I could have done with that!

Constable Davidson's dark eyes caught me in an intense stare. Terror swirled through me. I was in more trouble than I'd thought. How much did they know? I had to be stronger than them. I sucked in my cheeks, raised my chin, and looked him right in the eye. "I don't know anything about that." At least it was true.

"Can you explain why we have reports of you exiting Mr. Hunter's apartment on Saturday night at about ..." Constable Jeffries, on the other side of me, checked his notebook, "eleven o'clock?"

I was surrounded by enemy fire. These guys were good.

"Uh, I helped Hunter out sometimes. Carried in his purchases. But I wasn't there Saturday. Your sources must have got the wrong night."

I knew my excuse sounded lame, but now I could never admit that I'd been in Hunter's place that night. They'd think I'd stolen his money!

"OK, son. If you're sure you didn't see anything." Constable Jeffries put a beefy hand on my shoulder and squeezed. He was so close I could smell his aftershave. "Nice to hear that you help out your neighbors."

I cringed inside.

Constable Davidson gave me his card. "In case you remember something important," he said.

After my father shut the door, he gave me a searing, skeptical look. "Are you sure you're not involved? Hunter hardly needed help carrying anything."

"Dad! I'm not a thief!" Yet I could feel my face heating up and I couldn't look at Mom when I said it.

"We believe you, Flynn," Mom said quickly, putting a hand on Dad's arm. "But if you ever want to talk about anything, we're here for you."

"Thanks, Mom." As if I didn't feel bad enough. I gave her a smile, and thought about how I was going to get back at Tony.

* * *

I CORNERED TONY AS SOON AS I COULD at school the next day, after first period. Everyone was noisy so we could talk without much chance of being heard.

"Why did you tell the cops about me?" I would have pinned Tony to the lockers, but he was two times bigger than me.

"What'd you take?"

"What do you mean?"

"You know what I mean."

"No, I don't."

Tony looked at me long and hard. "You didn't take that cash?"

I couldn't believe that Tony was asking me this. "What are you talking about?"

"Shh."

Two girls bounced to the locker beside us. Tony pulled me away from them by the shirt and shoved me up against the water fountain.

"If you didn't take that cash, who did?" Tony tapped two fingers against my shoulder, pushing me backward until the fountain jabbed me in the back.

"How should I know?" I thought briefly of that guy with the cardboard box. He was getting on the elevator as I was heading into Hunter's. The box had been big enough. Maybe he was the thief, but I sure wasn't. I mean, I had just taken a few beers, five bucks, and a ribbon. That hardly counted for anything, right?

"You know what I took," I whispered, moving off the fountain and rubbing my back. "Beer. That's it. I had nothing to do with anything else. I didn't even know he had died until Tanya told me about it."

"Yeah, you did look surprised."

"Of course, I did. Geez, Tony."

I didn't like where this conversation was going. I was supposed to be the one accusing Tony of snitching. Instead he was accusing me of taking the money. For some reason, that really bothered me. Because I wasn't a thief, just an opportunist. Right?

* * *

OVER THE NEXT FEW DAYS, I fingered the cop's card in my pocket until it was tattered. And I thought a lot about Hunter, probably dead while I was stealing his beer. My mother was still looking desperately for her ribbon—in between giving me sideways glances. Dad just glared at me.

I didn't know what to do about Hunter. Tell the cops about the guy with the box? He could have been the thief. But then they would know that I'd been lying. Maybe they would think I was working with the real thief. The idea gnawed away at me, but I couldn't help Hunter now. He was dead. Yet I could do something for Mom.

That night, I dug the ribbon out of the ground and washed it the best I could in the bathroom with the door locked. It was still crumpled and wet, and it smelled like a sewer, although it was mostly clean.

Mom was doing crosswords at the kitchen table, munching green grapes. Dad was across the hall, playing dominoes. I sneaked into the living room, listening for any movement from the kitchen. I slinked around the fish tank and the coffee table to her chair, then I reached into her purse, which was on the rug beside her chair.

I couldn't return the five dollars yet, but I promised myself that I would pay her back, in time. After all that had happened, I vowed that I would and I meant it.

"Flynn? What are you doing in my purse?"

Her voice sounded hurt, and her eyes were pinched and sad.

"I'm just …" What could I say?

She waited with her mouth turned down and her eyebrows ruffled in disappointment.

"I …"

Would the truth hurt?

"I'm returning your ribbon." I squared my shoulders and faced her.

"What?"

"I'm so sorry, Mom. I took your ribbon to give to someone else. Someone who doesn't even care about me. I'm really sorry. Here."

I thrust the soggy, crushed ribbon at her.

She took in a sharp breath. Slowly, she reached for the ribbon. "Flynn!" She frowned then began to smile. I don't think she knew whether to yell at me or give me a crushing hug.

Mom took it from me and rubbed it between her fingers. She didn't seem to care that it was wrinkled and wet.

"I'm glad you returned it," she said. "That took courage, Flynn."

That wasn't so bad. I let my breath out. "I'm glad I returned it, too."

I smiled back at her, relieved that she wasn't yelling at me. Then Hunter snuck into my thoughts. I had to make it up to him as well.

I thought about the $5,000. Someone had stolen that money. Hunter would have wanted it back for his daughter. Maybe I could help. Maybe the police could catch the real thief. Even if I did get in trouble, I had an opportunity—an opportunity to help.

"Mom?" I hesitated.

"Yes?" She folded her arms and tilted her head as if she would be able to understand me better from another angle.

I gulped in a deep breath then spoke. "Remember when you said we could talk about anything?" She nodded. "Well, I think we'd better talk now. You, me, Dad—and the cops."

Stern Paddle

Sidney

Apt. 1219

THE CANOE SCRATCHED THE SANDY BOTTOM and thumped into a massive gray rock, almost knocking me off my seat.

"Sidney, whatcha doing up there, girl?" my father called from the stern.

"Oops!" Thoughts of Clive, back in the city without me, burst like tiny popping bubbles. I heaved my tired legs out of the canoe and got two chilly bootfuls of water for my trouble.

"Cold!" I yelled.

Dad laughed, even when I splashed him. I began to pull the canoe over to the sandy patch where we should have landed.

"Made it," I said after I yanked the canoe partway onto the bank. Our campsite looked like a luxury hotel after the long daytrip.

My legs were stiff from sitting so long, and my arms were sore from pulling the paddle. I wanted to collapse on the sand, but I straddled the bow of the canoe to steady it for my father.

"Oh, I'm an old man." He groaned as he stepped over the gunnels.

"Can't keep up with me?" I teased.

"Humph." He threw the two daypacks far up onto shore with one easy toss. "Not too old to get a fire started before you can unpack our supper." The skin around his eyes crinkled.

"You're on."

I was too tired to help get supper, but I was too hungry not to. My father had chosen a challenging route for us. A cluster of portages—the longest took over an hour. At least we hadn't had to carry much. Most of the gear had stayed back at the camp.

My father headed to the fire pit with the daypacks, after he pulled the canoe up. I hurried up the slope of rock and earth to the pine tree that held the food pack, and began, once again, to think about Clive.

The movie had started it. "Come on, Sidney. I can't go to a girl flick," he'd said, flashing those huge brown eyes at me and smiling innocently.

I'd frowned, but he'd leaned in for a kiss. His hair had fallen in waves against my cheek and his rough stubble had given me shivers. One kiss and I had lost myself in the dark curve of his lashes, only coming to my senses later at a disturbing David Cronenberg flick. I was beginning to see that Clive ran my life.

A hunger pain, growling and kicking at my stomach, brought me back to the forest. I untied the yellow nylon rope from around a branch and lowered the food pack. I could hear my father chopping wood. Clink. Clunk. Sticks of kindling clattered over the rocks.

I knew the routine. Birch bark and cedar to start the fire. Bigger pieces of the dry cedar log we'd found. Finally larger strips of hardwood—birch and maple.

My father had taught me everything I knew about camping. How pitching your tent in a low spot meant you woke up in a puddle after a rainstorm. How eating bananas made the mosquitoes ruthlessly seek out your blood. And how to start a campfire with dry softwood.

Clive hadn't wanted me to go camping. "You'd rather canoe with your old man than hang out in the city with me?" His face had gone red before he pulled away.

"My dad is making me go. Please, Clive. You know how it is." I had grabbed for his hand, hoping that he wouldn't discover my small white lie.

I couldn't explain it to Clive, and I couldn't give up the trip. Why choose my father's company over his? Because of the peaceful green-black forests, the calm purple of the evening sky, the rebellious white-gray rocks that jammed through the earth. And because Clive couldn't come.

The beauty of the lakes and the forests recharged me. Reminded me that the world could be open and beautiful. Not like my Building, which squeezed us so tight together that we could hear each other sweat. The Building made me dislike people because up close they seemed just as hopeless, and helpless, as me. But in the wilderness, my problems melted away from me like lumps of butter in a hot frying pan. My lungs expanded to fill my chest, and I could laugh with my father.

Not that I couldn't laugh with Clive. I had laughed with him through those staged wrestling shows that he liked so much. I had laughed with him when I beat his friend Ernie in a beer-chugging contest. Clive and I had shared a lot of fun—when we did what he wanted.

I dug further into the food pack for the freeze-dried stew and dumpling mix. My hands felt each bag to discover the contents. Pancake powder, pasta, raisins, granola bars. When I found the granola bars, I pulled them out for a little snack. My father might finish the fire before I gathered the food, but my stomach was crying out and supper was still way off.

The September air was cooling down fast as the sun edged closer to the hills, and I was getting cold in my T-shirt. In the east, dark clouds loomed, but they were still too far away to be much of a threat.

I bit into a granola bar and my stomach gratefully started to digest the first few crumbs. I was just searching for my jacket when I heard a dull thud then a gurgling sound. The sounds were strange, and I couldn't place them. Not a chipmunk. Not a loon. Another sound came. A cry of pain, strangled into a murmur.

"Dad?"

The wind stopped. The trees stilled. The birds were silent. A passing cloud threw a shadow over the camp. I dropped my granola bar and raced around our tent, just missing one of the nearly invisible cords that held out the side.

I saw his face first, white as a cloud. His red hair even more fiery than usual. The axe had dropped to the ground.

Blood squirted over the neat pile of kindling. My heart pounded the taps of a woodpecker beating on a tree.

"I ... cut ... my ... thumb." A grimace of pain flashed across his face, and I remembered my father's weakness—how he fainted at the sight of blood.

I grabbed Dad's arm. He was holding his thumb with his other hand, trying to stop the flow of blood. I couldn't tell how bad it was.

"Let me see."

My father sunk to his knees in the sandy dirt of the campsite. Somewhere nearby a red squirrel began to scold us. A chickadee called out. The wind found its voice again. My father opened his hand so we could both see the damage.

I held back a gasp and shut my eyes. "Oh!"

His thumb was sliced lengthwise from the middle down into the fleshy muscle of his hand. A river of blood pulsed through the wound. My head grew dizzy and my stomach tightened.

Dad squeezed his thumb with his other hand. He leaned into a tree. "We can't stay, Sidney. We have to paddle out tonight."

Paddle out tonight. With no supper. After a long day of hiking and canoeing. Hours of paddling in the dark.

"OK." I stared at my shoes. How would I paddle all that way?

Dad lifted my chin with one finger, his hand still clasped over the cut. "We'll make it."

"I know," I said, trying to sound convinced.

Dad straightened his shoulders and stood up. "Get me the first aid kit. And I'll need a strip of cloth. Just rip a piece off one of my shirts. A clean piece, if you can find one. I'll tie it around to try to stop the bleeding."

"Right away."

His orders comforted me, and I hurried to follow them.

* * *

ONCE HIS THUMB WAS WRAPPED and bandaged, I made up a bottle of powdered orange drink for us to share, and we had a quick supper of crackers and cheese, peanuts and raisins. I noticed that Dad hardly ate, although I couldn't get enough. He drank plenty of what he called snake-bite medicine. It was the apricot brandy that he'd brought in a wineskin.

"Let's pack up," he said as I screwed the lid on the plastic jar of peanuts and raisins. But he didn't move.

Dad's face was pale. His eyes had a shiny, glazed-over stare. I silently questioned him. Pack up? Wouldn't we leave it all here—the tent, sleeping bag and pads, and everything else that we didn't need for the trip? Couldn't we come back and get it later? I looked down at his thumb where the blood had soaked through the bandage. Maybe he was going into shock. Maybe he wasn't thinking straight.

He caught my look. "It's not too bad. I can pack."

I knew that he sometimes pushed himself too hard, but I said nothing. We began to pack the camp.

My stomach had a tight knot like a stone in it. I tackled the things outside the tent while Dad did the inside so he could sit down. He handed the sleeping bags and pads out to me then began to take down the tent. I packed the knapsacks—one for food and cooking equipment, the other for everything else. I had to pack properly because we had one short portage to hike, but at least most of the trip out was paddling.

I caught my father resting beside the half-finished tent, his hand holding up his head.

"I'll do it," I said. "You rest."

How would I get him out if he passed out? He was huge compared to me.

Dad lay down with his head on a rock. "The first-aid kit, Sidney? The pain is ... bad." His voice sounded so calm, but his forehead was knotted.

I raced over to the packed knapsack and pulled things out, looking for the first-aid kit. Why hadn't I put it on top? I couldn't make any mistakes. I had to be smarter.

The sun was starting to sink behind the hills of trees as I finished packing the canoe. It was a cedar-strip—light enough for me to carry short distances. My father and I had made it in his friend Bert's garage on weekends. That was before Clive. With Dad and Bert, I made the mold, stapled on the strips of cedar, built the seats and gunnels, and fiberglassed. Even now, the warm shine of the wood was a comfort.

I guided my father to the stern of the canoe. My father always took the stern—he was heavier and better at steering. I always sat in the bow, although I knew how to stern paddle.

"No, Sidney." He motioned toward the bow. "You'll have to take the stern. I'll try to help as much as I can."

Me, stern paddle? With the weight of my father and the packs against me? Could I do it?

"OK," I said. My heart tightened into a fist inside my chest.

With shaking hands, I adjusted the packs so the canoe would be balanced with his weight in the front. As we pushed off from the rocks rounded smooth by water, a white-throated sparrow called out. My favorite bird was saying goodbye. I was leaving too soon. I stepped into the stern. The birdcall turned into a cruel laugh.

* * *

DAD STARTED OUT PADDLING. He called out steering tips from the bow. "You should be able to keep your paddle on one side. Don't keep switching sides. Use the J-stroke."

My shoulders soon began to ache. I tried to remember the lessons my father had taught me. I knew the J-stroke. After experimenting for a few minutes, I managed to find a groove and relax into the even rhythm of paddling.

Dad paddled for a while, but I could tell he was in pain by the awkward way he held the paddle. After an hour, he dropped it in the canoe. I watched, afraid, as his head began bobbing up and down with the rhythm of waking and sleep. Was he falling asleep or passing out? I tried to paddle faster. And I began to sing. I sang to keep my father awake, and to drive away my fear. Every song I knew. Songs from summer camps, school, and even the radio. From Kumbaya to the latest pop song, I sang them all.

Every so often I'd stop singing to check the map, which was usually my father's job. I tried to match the shapes on the map to the curves of the lake, but as dusk closed around us I couldn't tell the islands from the points of land.

When I was thoroughly lost and beginning to stare around at the blanket of forest that looked the same in every direction, my father woke long enough to re-direct me.

"You're off course. To the left of that island then straight on."

With relief, I followed his directions. What would I do without him?

Once we rounded the head of the island, I almost yelped when I saw the familiar narrowing that led to the next lake. Deer Lake, it was called on the map, with the camp for kids clearly marked.

By the time we'd passed the camp—now closed for the season—the heavy clouds that had haunted us from a distance all afternoon had settled overhead. Then darkness hit, as black as the wings of a crow. The forest cast gloomy shadows along the ink of the lake. Again, I couldn't tell which direction to go.

The wind came up loud enough to stop my singing. Large waves began to crash against the bow and push the canoe back the way we had come. I gripped the gunnels to steady us. Cold water splashed my hands and arms as each wave threatened to flood the canoe.

I couldn't do this. Who was I kidding? I was small—hardly a hundred pounds. I needed help.

"Wake up, Dad," I yelled.

Nothing. Panic welled up in me and threatened to explode out of my throat.

"Dad! Wake up! Da-a-ad!" I yelled so loud my voice echoed back to me from the empty hills.

"Huh?"

"Dad!" I was never so glad to see him awake. "Get the rain gear. In the top of the pack. No. Behind you."

He was still groggy but he managed to do it. We threw the raingear on over our wet clothes. My hands were shaking as I zipped my coat up to my chin. There were still two more lakes to go.

* * *

I KEPT PADDLING THOUGH MY ARMS ACHED. Waves pressed harder at me. Then, from some small corner of my mind, I remembered something—head for shore. A canoe was no match for storm winds, even on a small lake.

Taking the long way in and around each bay, we hugged the shoreline. I pulled the canoe through the next lake, closer and closer to the portage. I peered at the silhouettes of curves and hillsides against the night sky, desperate for a sign that I was going the right way. Every time I looked at Dad, sleeping more than waking now, my breath caught in my throat.

Just as my arms could no longer stretch forward for another stroke, I glimpsed the sign that marked the portage. It was a fluke. A tiny glimmer of yellow among the murky trees.

The rain had held back for me. The wind was dying. I was going to make it—to the portage at least.

"Thank you," I whispered.

The wilderness was harsh and unforgiving, but it wasn't really so different from my home in the city in some ways. The indifference of the strangers that were my neighbors in the Building. The unexpected hazards in the underground and the stairwells. Yet Clive had shown me another world in the city. Once he had walked me through the secret paths of the city valleys, surprising me with a picnic basket, a single red rose, and a grassy spot where we could be alone. Another time, we went to an Ethiopian restaurant where the waiter had explained that when we shared a plate of food we could never betray one another. Was that true?

Dad woke up long enough to paddle the final stretch, and I was glad for the help. Never before had I pulled so much weight alone. At the portage, he stumbled out of the canoe and onto the bank. He forgot to pull the canoe up on shore and headed for the nearby forest.

He's just going to pee, I told myself, although I wasn't sure.

I stepped out into the water without caring if my boots got any wetter and pulled the canoe onto shore. I lifted out the backpacks and watched uneasily for Dad to return. After a few minutes, I couldn't wait any longer. I hurried into the forest after him.

The night owned the forest more completely than the lake, and I couldn't find a sign of him. Every whisper of a leaf, every shadow of a rock made me shiver. I wanted to find my father and get out of there.

"Dad? Dad?"

No answer. I wished I'd brought a flashlight.

"Dad?" I called more sharply. I craned my neck to catch a glimpse of him, my whole body tight with hope and fear.

He hadn't gone far, although every second was like a minute until I found him. I tried to hug him, but he pulled away and began walking in circles around a tree, staring up into the leaves and muttering. Maybe the pain was worse. I knew that the sight of blood made him faint but could he become delirious? I grabbed his face in my hands and tried to make him see me.

"Dad, you OK?" He was always so strong. So capable. What was wrong?

He looked at me, confused, and said nothing.

My heart sank into my boots. This couldn't happen. Dad couldn't be so weak. I needed him. I wanted him back to normal. I wanted him to take care of me now. I wanted him to make this whole nightmare end.

If only Clive had come. He would have figured out a plan. Maybe that was why I liked him. Because he took control. Yet no one was here to help me. I was responsible now. For Dad. For myself. For everything.

I led my father back to the canoe with firm steps. I would take charge, like Clive always did. Push back at everything that was pushing at me. I had to.

I grabbed a flashlight and some granola bars from the packs and shoved them in the pocket of my raincoat. Then I left the two packs in plain sight at the side of the trail. We would have to come back for them later.

With a jerky swing, I tried to get the canoe upside-down over my head. It crashed back down on a rock and I cringed, thinking of how we had lovingly crafted it. Three times I tried, until I finally got it up on my shoulders.

"Come on, Dad," I said breathlessly as I struggled under the heavy load. If only he would follow me over the portage.

Even after my eyes had adjusted to the dim forest, I could see little without a flashlight. The hike wasn't too long, but my shoulders ached from the weight of the canoe and my legs buckled every time I stumbled over a root. Then Dad wouldn't hold a flashlight steady on the trail, and he wandered into the woods instead of following the path.

I left the canoe propped against a tree and took Dad by the hand. The flashlight jerked and trembled over the path as I pulled him along.

The trail seemed much longer going out than it did coming in. It refused to end. Finally I heard the slap of waves on rock. Then I caught a glimpse of water through the trees and felt the cold lakeside wind on my cheeks. Shipeau Lake. The biggest lake, but it was the last one. When we arrived at the end of the portage, I sat my father down with one of the flashlights and a granola bar.

"Now don't move. OK, Dad?"

He nodded his head, but he didn't answer. Did he even understand? He had lost a lot of blood. I shined my flashlight on his hand and saw the soaked red bandage.

Without stopping to catch my breath, I ran back up the trail as fast as I could to get the canoe, the flashlight beam bouncing on the path ahead of me. I hoped that Dad wouldn't get into trouble while I was gone.

By the time I got the canoe back on my shoulders, it felt heavier than before. All I could hear was the sound of my own stumbling footsteps and my breath chugging in and out of my mouth. Each step shot pain through my shoulders, and I was sweating in spite of the cold. Then, the land sloped down and I could hear the lap of the waves.

"Dad?" I called as I threw the canoe down by the water.

He hadn't wandered away, but he didn't answer me. He was sitting still, with the granola bar in his hand, unopened. In the eerie glow of the flashlight, his skin was too white, his eyes vacant.

I guided Dad to the bow of the canoe then stuffed his uneaten granola bar into my mouth. Hunger roared louder inside me but I didn't even stop to take a swallow from my water bottle. Instead, I thrust the canoe out into the dark lake and shoved off. One big lake to cross.

* * *

IN THE NARROW CHANNEL, I SEARCHED with my eyes and the flashlight until I could see the first curve into the lake. I didn't need the map for this part of the journey—I knew it by heart.

Yet as I rounded the curve, rain began to fall. Gentle drops that were almost welcome, then harder drops that prickled my face and hands. The wind was blowing toward me. I squinted ahead but all I could see were millions of raindrops battering the water's surface.

I stopped paddling, and the canoe began to drift backward. How could I do this with all of nature lashing out at me?

My father sat slumped in the front of the canoe.

"Dad, can you help me paddle?" I said with a sob, sure that he wouldn't answer me.

A grunt in reply. Nothing more. I squeezed my eyes shut and begged that an unseen force would help me out of this mess.

The canoe rocked on the growing waves, travelling faster and faster the wrong way. What should I do? Try to find shelter? What would my father do?

I looked at the waves washing into the canoe, the trees brushing the sky, the rain hurtling down. A power far greater than me was against us.

I couldn't take the punishment anymore. Everything and everyone was out to get me, and I was tired of it. Clive bossed me around. So did Dad. Now this angry sky was out to get me, too. But this time I was ready to fight back.

I screamed, "You can't push me around!" My words foolish. Yet something inside me was stronger for saying them. Peaceful, in spite of the storm.

I picked up my paddle and began once again to force the canoe through the water. Dip, pull, lift, and swing. Dip, pull, lift, and swing. Just keep moving. Prove what I could do on my own.

The rain pelted harder, turned into needles. I paddled for what felt like hours—past the point, between the islands, and around the final curve into a narrow bay.

I had almost made it. Now the wind was at my side. The waves were smaller. I could open my eyes a little wider and see where I was going.

On the other side of the bay I could make out the beach, the dock, the rangers' office, and a row of cars. I could see a light in the office.

My hands were crunched into painful claws from gripping the paddle for so long. I paddled a little harder, pulling until my muscles ached more than I knew they could. One stroke at a time across the bay.

"We're almost there, Dad."

If he heard me, he didn't show it.

Finally the canoe scraped over the tiny pebbles of the shore. I stepped out into the lake in my soggy boots.

"We made it!" I yelled out to the gray swirling sky. Then I turned to my father. "Come on, Dad."

I held my father's arm to steady him. Blood dripped through the bandage and splashed into the water. It spread out with feathery tentacles until a wave washed it away.

Then my father spoke. "Sidney?" He squeezed my hand with his good hand like he was afraid to ever let it go. "What happened? How did I get here?"

I squeezed his hand right back. Saw his eyes clearer than they had been since the accident.

"You're going to be all right, Dad."

My muscles ached, my teeth chattered with the cold, but a lightness came upon me. We had made it. I had paddled Dad out by myself. I had found my way, carried the canoe, and battled the wind, rain, darkness, hunger, and time. And no one had told me what to do.

Stinks Like Flowers

David

Apt. 1407

I COULD SEE THE CEMETERY through the Jackal's bedroom window. The Jackal stood between me and the open window, blaring his new tune on his red electric guitar. He'd made me do the vocals.

"Get up! Stand up on your two feet!" I sang off key and out of time. "Don't you know, we've got so much to beat?"

I gave the Jackal his name because he stayed up late and because he liked to prowl the clubs at night, just to check out the scene. And because his real name was Hubert. The Jackal was aiming to be the next electric-guitar superstar.

"'Cause we can do it all to-ge-e-ther! Yeah! We can do it all to ..."

I stopped and let the Jackal go on solo. His hair had swung over half his face and his long fingers were grinding out the tune with all he had. But the cemetery kept tugging me away from him.

The Jackal lives five blocks away from the Building, in a house that backs onto the cemetery. When we were younger, we tunnelled behind the huge oak tree in his yard and into the cemetery to make a secret cave. Now I couldn't stop staring at the rows of stones, although I hadn't set foot in there for six months. Not since Dad had been buried.

"Hey, Davie-boy." The Jackal had stopped playing and was waving a hand in front of my eyes. "You going to do that on stage?"

I snapped back into the room. "Huh?"

"You'll never be my lead singer that way."

"Wouldn't I have to be able to sing in tune to do that?" I stared over his shoulder.

The Jackal followed my glance out the window, over his huge grassy backyard, and into the cemetery.

"I've been thinking," he began. "Maybe we should dig up a few bodies out there. Take all the old rings and jewels to sell." His smirk showed he was joking, but sometimes the Jackal did do some weird stuff. "We'd be rich. Then we could quit school and do some real living. What do you think, David?"

"Real living sounds good, whatever that is."

The Jackal clapped me on the back. "Yeah! Hotel suites, music, and girls! Just think of it!"

I smiled. Girls would be good. The Jackal fixed me with his cool, dark stare but my eyes slipped back to the window. I couldn't help it.

I'd stopped sleeping for a while after Dad died and I hadn't eaten much. Now I was better, although I hated that he died, and how. The long illnesses, unexpected recoveries, and sudden relapses. All those tubes coming out of his arms and nose, and the machines pumping the air in and out of his lungs. His papery skin and sunken eyes. The annoying grief counsellors. The worst had been the smell. His room at the hospice had stunk like dead flowers. I had to breathe through my mouth the whole time.

The Jackal blasted me with a few licks at full volume.

I jumped. "Huh?"

"You're set on a break. I'll raid the fridge." He swung his guitar strap over his shoulder and set his guitar tenderly on the stand.

"I'm not hungry."

"I know, skin-and-bones, but I am."

I couldn't eat. I couldn't sing. I couldn't do anything. What I really wanted to do was ask Dad one question. Why? Why did he have to get AIDS? Why did he have to die? What was I going to do if Mom got sick? But that was more than one question.

When they'd talked to us about condoms and safe sex at school today, some joker flipped a condom over to me and said, "Your dad should have used one of these." I was so mad I could have spit.

Dad had sworn it was his hospital visit in '86. Mom still said it didn't matter how he got AIDS or what other people thought about it. She said we just had to deal with his illness, his death, and her being HIV positive. But she was wrong. It mattered to me.

The Jackal brought back fried chicken, cold pizza, two pops, and a bag of popcorn. He laid it out on his bed and offered me a slice.

I shook my head at the pizza but I pulled myself away from the window for a drink. I owed the Jackal that much. Because after Dad had gotten sick, some guys at school had started to wink at me and call me pretty boy. The

Jackal had to hold me back. Were they stupid enough to think that only gay men got AIDS? Everyone else gave me those scared, mean eyes that said, "We know your Dad's got it. Don't give it to us." Everyone except the Jackal. His eyes never changed. That's how I knew he was my real friend.

* * *

I HAD NEVER EXPECTED TO REALLY TALK to Dad's ghost until one night after a soccer game. Mom had made me stay in soccer. "He would have wanted it," she'd said. Funny, but soccer was one of the only times that I still felt alive. That and being with the Jackal.

It was the last game in a tournament west of the city. We lost four to two. After the game, one rear tire on the car was low. Too low to drive. Slushy-wet rain was starting to fall. Mom put her hands on her hips and let out a string of curses that I would never repeat.

She wasn't like a normal mom. She would swear if she wanted to and she didn't mind if I did it either, as long as I didn't swear at a person. I could curse cars, trucks, doors, the weather, but not people. Dad had never let me swear at anything, but he couldn't say much about it now.

Twenty minutes later, a tow-truck driver was pumping up our tire.

"Either it's a slow leak or someone took the air out for a joke," he said in between smacks of his gum. "There's a garage two blocks over where you can check the tire for leaks. Just so you don't get a flat on the highway."

I looked at Mom with a meaningful stare, but she didn't notice. I knew a couple of guys on the team who would do this. Maybe Willis or Richardson. Somehow, the news about my dad had gotten to them, too. Why wouldn't they leave me alone? I wished the Jackal went out for soccer.

The garage was in a small gas station. It didn't look open, but we pulled in anyway. Old cars crowded the parking lot. There was hardly room for my mother to drive in, but she made us fit.

The office was filled with soccer trophies, photos of hot cars that looked as if they were ripped out of an old calendar, and pictures of saints with halos over their heads. In a greasy coverall, the owner was talking loudly on the phone in Greek. The room was dirty, run down, and needed painting—depressing, like the Building. And it stunk like car exhaust because the door to the garage was open.

There were two men waiting in the office as well. One was sitting on one of the chairs lined up under the window. His hair was gray and he was wearing one of those jackets with a nametag on it. Stan—that was what his tag said. The other was standing. He was a bit younger, skinny, and his ears stuck out from under his baseball cap. Both looked too old to be interesting.

Then the guy behind the desk was off the phone and Mom was talking to him in the garage. I was just hanging, so I couldn't help but listen to the skinny guy talking to Stan.

"I couldn't tell ya whether I'm Scottish or Irish. I went back to New Brunswick—where I'm from—to find my family."

"Family's important." Stan nodded.

"Yep. I tried to look them up in the cemetery while I was there, but they weren't about to talk to me. Now I'll never know whether I'm Scottish or Irish."

I knew he was just kidding about ghosts talking to him. That wasn't the weird thing. The weird thing was what the guy named Stan said next.

He said, "If you want them to talk to you, you don't go there in the daytime. You got to go at night. Alone. Then they'll talk to you."

I slid my eyes sideways to see if there was any hint of humor in his face, but there wasn't. He just looked still and serious at the skinny guy.

The skinny guy began to shuffle nervously from foot to foot and sneak weird looks at Stan. "I get ya."

Stan used this as an invitation to talk some more. "Yeah, you gotta go alone at night. Walk among the tombstones and pray that the one you want to talk to will come and see you. If you see something sneaking out from behind a tree and feel a tap on your shoulder, then you know."

"Oh, jeez," said the skinny guy, shuffling about more now. "That's when I'm outta there. No way."

He scuttled out of the office and into the gray drizzle as if he had something important to do, but I knew he was trying to get away from the spooky talk.

Mom came out of the garage then with the mechanic.

"Come on, David. I need your help," she called to me.

I followed them outside.

Mom passed me the keys. "We're going to do a quick check without taking the tire off," she explained. "We'll look for the nail while you drive slowly backward. Can you handle that?"

"Sure!"

Glad for a chance to be behind the wheel, I rolled back, watching my mother's hand in the driver's mirror show me when to stop and go. When she stuck her head right under the car, I braked so hard she bumped her head.

"Be careful!" I yelled at her.

They found nothing. Someone must have let the air out. It could have been one of the guys on the team. Or maybe it was Tony, from the Building. He had been giving me mean sideways looks. Anyway, I wouldn't trust anyone from the Building, especially after the way they hounded Petra last summer—for a lousy twenty bucks!

While Mom talked some more to the mechanic, I went back and fingered the soccer trophies, pretending they were mine, but I was thinking about what Stan had said. About how he had said it—as if it were true. As if he could read my mind. Then Stan started to speak.

"What I said before, boy, it's on the level, sure enough."

I looked at him then. He seemed so ordinary. So I gathered my courage and asked, "How do you know it's true?"

He smiled, wiggled his false teeth around in his mouth, and said, "Because I've done it. Talked to my own mama one year to the day after she died. That was on a visit to her grave. And my brother, well, he called me on the telephone the day after he died to tell me about some money he had hidden in his apartment, in the wall behind the light switch. I guess he didn't want the next people to find it. Sure enough, when I took that light switch apart, it was there. Right where he told me to look."

He must have been pulling my leg, but a shiver crept through me. Stan was still looking serious, so I just said, "Oh." What was I supposed to say to something like that?

"Most of the dead don't walk to the cemetery," he continued.

"I know that." Maybe this guy was just a loser.

Stan ignored me. "Some of them get lost. Can't find their way."

I wondered why ghosts had to hang out in cemeteries. Couldn't they be anywhere else?

Mom called me then. "No leak, David, time to go."

I'd lost my chance to find out more, but I knew I would go to the cemetery—just to see if it was true.

* * *

AT 11:30 THAT NIGHT, I SNEAKED down the hall, away from Mom's soft snores. I shut our heavy metal apartment door without even a click. No problem. Half an hour to get into position. I figured that midnight was the best time to talk to ghosts.

I put the collar of my jean jacket up against the wind and any strange people that might be lurking on the city streets. When I got to the Jackal's house, I scooted around the side and climbed over the fence. My feet landed with a crunch on the dry leaves that were bunched up against his fence.

Gloomy blackness closed in on me. I stood for a long time behind the Jackal's house, shaking a bit and sweating, even in the cool night air. I stared up at his darkened window and listened to the wind whirling around the headstones and rustling the leaves in the trees. Little animals that I'd never noticed during the day scurried from stone to stone. I wished that the Jackal was with me, but Stan had said to go alone.

Then I started down the rows, thinking of all the horror shows I'd ever seen. The moon shone through the tree branches, making strange shadows, but I saw no ghosts. I tried to read the names and dates on the tombstones in the dark and almost cried over each grave. This sappy sobbing thing had taken me over ever since Dad had died.

I was heading to Dad's grave—the place I had been avoiding since I watched the coffin sink into that dark pit months ago. I hadn't even come when the stone was placed, but I knew where the grave was. The spot still haunted me in my dreams. Sixth from the end of the row near a bush that had been blooming red flowers on that day. I sat facing his gray rectangular stone, but not on his grave. I couldn't step on him.

Thomas Duncan MacKay
Beloved husband to Margaret Anne
Beloved father to David Thomas
May all lost souls find their way to eternal light.

Why did my mother put that on his tombstone? Maybe Dad was one of the ghosts who got lost on the way to the cemetery. Or maybe she was thinking about me. Or herself.

Dad wasn't there. I shivered and pushed away my disappointment and relief. What should I do next?

Then I remembered that Stan had said to pray. I'd never prayed before, but I'd seen other people do it, so I tried.

I got on my knees and mumbled into my folded hands. Private stuff about how I was worried about Mom and how I missed Dad and wanted to see him again. Then I lit a couple of matches because the rustling noises around me were spooky. I started wishing again that the Jackal were with me, but he was probably sleeping or jamming guitar in the dark with his headphones on. So I just sat and waited for Dad to come.

The thing that I didn't plan for was the wait. And that I fell asleep. And that Dad's ghost didn't appear. The worst was that I fell asleep on top of my father's grave.

I dreamed that I was deep in the ground with Dad. Buried alive, with him dead. Choking and suffocating on the dirt and stale air. With the maggots and worms and stink of crumbling flesh and bones. It smelled worse than the dead flowers in the hospice.

I woke with a scream. Tears had wet my cheeks. Someone was standing over me. A silhouette of a person outlined in the moonlight. Was it my father? Waiting for me to wake up? Waiting to give me the answers? To tell me why I had to suffer this life?

I had forgotten that the Jackal was like the animal I'd named him for. I had forgotten that he could sniff me out. He was a creature of the night. Not like me. I belonged in the daylight, but the night kept creeping toward me until I couldn't avoid it any more.

The Jackal squinted to read Dad's tombstone in the light of the moon. He was wearing his usual ripped blue jeans and black leather jacket. "What's up?"

I wiped the tears from my cheeks and told the Jackal about Stan and how he had said he could talk to ghosts.

The Jackal looked at me, but his eyes didn't change. He didn't get that look of pity even though he saw me weak. Not strong like him.

"Awwh, there's no ghosts here," he said. "Just a bunch of dead guys. Let's beat it."

We did. I pretended to trip over the bones of a dead guy on the way out, and the Jackal laughed. I didn't want him to think I was soft.

* * *

I KNEW I WOULD TRY AGAIN. I had to. But it didn't happen how I thought it would.

The next Saturday, the Jackal and I were on our way to the arcade in the row of stores across from the Building. Mom was at the hospital for some tests. I was worrying about her and about how I would take care of myself and her if she got sick.

"I'm going to whip your butt in Kick-Off," the Jackal said, trying to trip me as we passed the tattoo place. Kick-Off was a great two-person soccer game at the arcade. It was the only kind of soccer that the Jackal ever played.

"Just try it," I said, jumping over his leg. Then I was remembering the times I had played Kick-Off with Dad. He had loved that game.

The tears gathering behind my eyes almost burst like rain clouds. Blood drained from my head. I probably looked as pale as a ghost.

The Jackal pulled me back from the storm. He nudged me and said, "Davie-boy? You see a ghost?"

We laughed together.

As we passed the big grocery store, the Jackal made the automatic doors open and shut. I stopped, laughed again, and made the doors open, too. The store manager, a grumpy woman with thick glasses, glared at us through the huge windows. The Jackal made to crack the window in front of her with a karate kick, and she ducked. We laughed some more, because his foot never even touched the window. She shook her fist at us and I made the doors open one more time.

It was when the doors were open that last time that I could feel Dad. I could tell it was him because it stunk like flowers, and I mean stunk. Not dead flowers like in the hospice, but fresh roses like he used to bring Mom, mixed with a bit of his own smell. It stunk so much that my eyes were watering buckets and my nose was running.

Of course, if you must know, there was a huge flower display just inside the automatic doors. Racks and stacks of roses, lilies, chrysanthemums, and mixed bunches in plastic wrappers. I suppose that I did get a good whiff of those flowers, but that doesn't matter.

Because, as I sobbed and wiped at my nose with the back of my hand, I wasn't so mad at Dad anymore. Somehow, in that moment, I forgave him for leaving us. It was the smell. Oh, that smell! I knew he was there. I knew that he was watching Mom and me. That he was with us and always would be. No matter what happened.

That day, after I let the Jackal beat me in Kick-Off, I bought the fullest bunch of red roses that I could find from the grocery store. The Jackal helped me pick them out.

"Let's do this right," I said.

We headed for the cemetery. The Jackal stopped at his place for his acoustic. It wouldn't be as good as the electric, but I didn't mind. I went ahead and set the flowers on Dad's grave.

"Let's rock this place!" the Jackal called out to me as he came strolling down through the thick tree trunks and rows of stones. He had his acoustic over one shoulder and a jar of water for the flowers.

"Thanks." I put the flowers in the jar and set it in the grass beside Dad's grave. The Jackal put one booted foot up on Dad's stone, rested the guitar on his leg, and did a quick tune up. I moved to the end of Dad's grave.

"One, two, three, four ..." the Jackal started.

It wouldn't bring Dad back or make Mom better. It wasn't enough to make a difference, but it was something.

"This one's for you, Dad," I said, then I began to sing, off key as usual.

As the Jackal and I worked the tune, the leaves rattled in the wind, and the green grass spread around us in every direction. Every so often the stink of the red roses drifted up to me on the breeze. I hoped Dad was listening, wherever he was.

Night Watch

Allie

Apt. 412

DAD HAD DISAPPEARED TWO MONTHS AGO, taking with him the last few strands that held my mother together. Now, Brad was squeezing out sideways through the apartment door, his bag on one shoulder and his hockey sticks aimed back at me.

"Bye," he yelled.

Mom, horizontal on the living-room couch, didn't answer.

I stood in the hall and watched the door slam. The apartment air was thick and close. I was alone with my mother.

I imagined Brad impatient in the elevator and then jogging out to his ride. A van packed with bulky guys like so much baggage, pulling away from the Building as fast as it could go. This time it was a weekend hockey tournament. At eighteen, it was easier for him to escape. So I kept the watch.

I avoided Mom. Instead, I purged the medicine cabinet. Only a few pills. Vitamins and cold tablets. I flushed them down the toilet. Just bandages left. She couldn't do much damage with those. Then I tiptoed to the hall closet. I checked her purse and all the coat pockets, searching for her hidden stash. I knew she made secret purchases.

Smuggled bottles of pills into the apartment. Yet I found nothing. Nothing except the letter hidden in my own coat pocket. I had it memorized.

> *"Allie White has been accepted for the Arts Abroad program in Paris. Please confirm her enrollment by completing the enclosed course selection form and accommodation application. We are delighted to have Allie join us."*

I shoved the paper deep down into my coat pocket. Paris, France, would never see me. How could I leave Mom for six months? Who would keep the watch?

The closet door squeaked as I slid it shut.

"That you, Allie?" Mom's voice was shaky and full of threatening tears. Her body so thin it almost flattened into the couch.

"Yeah, Mom."

"Oh." She sounded disappointed. I wondered who she wished I were.

* * *

SATURDAY NIGHT AFTER SUPPER, Mom was curled up on her bed, crying into a book, pretending to read. I had watched her cry many times. Sometimes, at the dinner table, silent tears ran down her face into her food. Other times, heavy sobs sneaked into my dreams, interrupting my sleep.

When I touched her shoulder, she startled. Her eyes were vacant. She struggled to recognize me.

"Allie?"

"Mom, I'm going out. Will you be OK?"

She nodded, and I could only hope it would be true.

I didn't want to leave her unguarded, unattended. Yet Cori had pressed me so hard. She had demanded my attention.

"You just have to come, Allie," she had pleaded through the phone. "Ron has dumped me and in the worst way. And now my dad is in a rage."

"What did you say to your dad?" I asked, knowing that Cori had self-destructed again.

"I just told him he was a fat, lazy slob who couldn't get out of bed without a hoist. Please, Allie, I can't bear to talk about it on the phone. I need to see you."

Cori was determined to harm herself. So was my mother, who tried on death each day like a new dress. Does this one fit? Which shade of gray suits me best?

I went to Cori's, three floors down in the Building. In the refuge of her pink bedroom, the door shut to her parents, Cori dragged out each of her problems and held them up to me for some kind of salvation. I nodded and listened. I didn't tell her about Paris. How could I?

She didn't know that in September I had written a 5,000-word essay on why I deserved a scholarship to Arts Abroad. She didn't know that our art teacher, Mr. Rimmold, had said that I had talent—real talent—for art. No one knew how much I wanted to go, and now I would never get the chance.

"And you know what his friend Steve said then?" Cori's bottom lip quivered as she barely paused for my answer.

"What did he say?"

"He said that ..." Cori talked on and on.

I watched Cori's cherry lips moving, anxious eyes fluttering, red hair flashing. Until the feeling crept up the back of my neck like a spider looking for a nesting site. Until I could no longer hear her words. Until the spider crawled into my ear, lodged in my brain, and began to spin a web. Something was wrong. Call it a premonition. I went home.

* * *

THE SILENCE IN THE APARTMENT told me nothing. No empty pill bottles in the garbage under the kitchen sink, but no soft sobs of grief either. I found her in her room, still on her bed, lying flat on her back like the dead. I tiptoed closer, listening for the quiet breath of life. Her silence drew me in, panicked me. Until I laid my ear upon her warm chest and felt the faint stirring of life.

Alive. For now. But what had she taken? Could she just be asleep? Not likely. My mother, who always woke with the birds after a restless sleep? Who cried out in the night, chased by whatever monsters, imagined or real, haunted her dreams? Who suffered sleeplessness for reasons I could not know?

I nudged her, but she lay still. The siren of a passing police car did not wake her. She had gone to the place the pills had taken her—the place of escape from herself.

I loathed Dad—could sink my teeth into his neck like some kind of animal. Because I should've escaped instead.

He had held my mother up until he could do it no longer, until something had snapped in him. But I was just sixteen, and duty should have made him stronger. Duty to Mom, duty to me, duty to Brad.

Dad used to find relief by eating whole pies or boxes of ice cream in front of the hockey game. His wide, round belly telling the story of his excess.

"Wahoo! Did you see that goal, Brad, my boy!"

And Brad answering his war-whoop.

Mom was like a fallen willow, lying on the couch in the light blue housecoat that signaled her mood. A pale white-blond beauty—so unlike my own tough, dark skin. Unlike Dad, Mom denied herself food, preferring to suffer the pang of hunger as punishment for a past I couldn't understand—didn't want to understand. Her whispers releasing secrets that my ears didn't want to hear.

"Why didn't you want me?" she would moan to the demons that haunted her. "Why didn't you love me? Please don't hurt me again."

Until Dad, too, had run from her demons, the demons that she fed us all. Banging around late at night, yelling, "I've had it!" and, "This is enough!" Thumping out the door and fleeing the scene. And Brad and I hearing it all from our beds.

"Oh, darling, don't leave me alone. I'll die without you."

I crouched for more than an hour beside my mother, quiet in her bed. If only she would moan or roll over. Give me a signal that I, too, could escape into sleep. She offered nothing. How could I go to Paris when I couldn't even leave Mom alone for a few hours?

Fighting my yearning for sleep, I set up watch at the kitchen table, down the hall from her. I got my sketchpad and charcoals, a large plastic cup with ice water, and an apple. Yet I couldn't draw. I couldn't eat or drink either. I could only wait for Mom to show a sign of life.

The night took on a pattern, a rhythm. I checked her breathing every fifteen minutes. Watched TV in between to stay awake. I listened for a soft sigh, a rustling, a sign of waking. It didn't happen. A sigh was too close to living for her. She could only manage a slow wisp of air in and a trickle out. Hardly awake. Hardly alive. Still hanging on.

I thought, she only took enough to taste death, not to meet it full on. She will be back.

Who else could understand, unless they lived it, too? I couldn't just phone for an ambulance every time I suspected. She was warning me, crying for help. Yet a nighttime trip to the hospital would be considered a betrayal. Mom could find many ways to punish those who crossed her. She controlled my every move, my every thought with a package of pills and a few well-delivered tears. Besides, the hospital would just release her after a few days or after a few weeks if it was bad. Soon after, the pattern of night watches would begin again.

* * *

THE ICE IN MY WATER HAD MELTED LONG AGO. The TV screen was gray. As the night lengthened into darkness, I had to do more.

I knelt beside Mom. She was still. If only I could will her to live. Maintain her heartbeat. Images of my mother, well and happy, ruled my thoughts, pumped through my veins, fuelled my sleeplessness. Like when she taught me to skate—pulled me around the ice rink, her boots solid and strong on the ice, my skates sliding without control. Or how she used to laugh—a high-pitched whinny through her nose.

Then I was connected, linked, with her. A cable of electricity pulled tight between us. Together, we would struggle with life and death.

I felt the haze of drugs as if I, too, had swallowed them, or maybe it was the haze of sleeplessness. I wanted to save her, to erase her suffering, to absorb it for her. If only I could help. Yet my mind became constricted by her sorrow. My limbs tied down with dead weights. Until, in a moment of weakness, sleep conquered me. On the floor beside her bed, I slept the sleep of exhaustion, the sleep of winter.

In my dream, I was floating, gliding, swallowed by water. A gentle rocking motion. My own voice singing, mocking childhood songs.

"Oh where, oh where has my mother gone? Oh where, oh where could she be?"

Then I swirled in the water to face Mom's bulging dead fish-eyes—lost in the land of endless sleep. Lost to those of us who still wished to live.

I tugged at her body. Struggled with her to the surface. Pulled her to shore where Dad and Brad watched without making any effort.

"Help us," I called. "Please."

Brad, ignoring me, twisted a hockey stick around and around in the ground as if he were grinding it into the heart of some cruel beast. Dad sneered, then spit into the sand beside me.

I woke then, trembling in the shadow of my dream, with my throat on fire, my skin burning, my head clouded. I had to get help, but Mom would never forgive me if I did. What to do? What if she never woke up?

With the ache of indecision choking me, I paced the floors. Kitchen. Living room. Bedroom. Kitchen. Living room. Bedroom. I breathed cool air into the fiery passages within me, the tension strangling tighter and tighter around me. I watched the night stretch on. I heard the silence of the night. Mom's silence.

Then, with the wonder of one who has lived through eternal blackness, I watched the night turn into day. People dotted the streets. Dogs barked out warnings. Birds twittered advice. An unexpected hunger grew within me. I denied myself food, although blueberry muffins lingered on the counter and orange juice beckoned from the fridge. How could I eat? What about Mom? I should be making tea and toast for her.

Fighting the hunger until noon, I sacrificed, keeping my steady watch. I made hopeful tea for her, guarding it until it grew cold. Then Brad, with hockey sticks like porcupine quills, swept in.

I met him at the door. "Brad, she's not awake yet. Should we call for help?"

Mom had never taken this long to wake up before.

Brad, smelling like sweat, couldn't let himself care. "Why don't you give her a bath? That's what Dad used to do."

Swinging his full shoulders around, he headed for bed.

Why didn't I think of that? I ran the bath. Not too cold, but cold enough to wake her. When the tub filled, I pulled the thin quilt off her. Like an intruder, I undressed her, repulsed yet fascinated by this woman, this stranger, my mother. I tugged her housecoat off. Pulled her nightgown over her head. Removed her socks but not her underwear.

Nudging Brad awake, I asked him to help carry Mom to the tub.

He refused to answer at first. Covered his head with his pillow and pretended not to hear. But he had no choice. He, too, was bound to protect her from herself.

"Cover her," he said when he saw her on the bed. I wrapped her in a sheet and grabbed one end, but Brad pushed me aside.

"I'll carry her myself."

He shouldered her with only a little trouble, then walked down the hall to the bathroom. Her one arm dangled behind him, white and frail. Brad dumped her in the bathtub, sheet and all, while I held her head to keep it from banging on the end of the tub. Then Brad, coolness in his eyes, turned from the shame and retreated again toward sleep. I let him go. What else could I do?

In the bath, I couldn't look away from her helplessness, a wisp of what she could be. Watching and waiting yet for a sign of life. For more than a breath.

With the first sweet groan, the first flutter of a finger, I saw with eyes wide open what I hadn't seen before. I saw the burden that I had come to accept. I had become my mother's caretaker. I could affect life and death. I had control. Yet a smaller, childish voice deep inside me whispered, "Just be my mother, and I will be your daughter."

Mom's eyes rippled open. I seized the chance.

"Mom, where is the bottle? What did you take?"

I leaned over her face, but didn't expect much of an answer. My mother moaned. Looked at me with glazed eyes. I couldn't help her.

Then she lifted a limp, dripping hand out of the bathwater and extended one shaking finger toward the shelf of towels above the toilet. She pointed the way for me. Maybe she was even asking for my help.

I jumped up, ready to take action. Felt between the soft folds. Flung the towels one by one onto the floor. Until a bottle crashed onto the linoleum and rolled against the cupboard.

Pain medication. I flipped the childproof lid off. The pills were almost gone. I flushed the rest of them. Put the empty bottle on the counter.

An idea nudged me as I wrapped a towel around Mom, helped her into her robe, and led her to the kitchen for some tea. It wasn't enough that Mom was OK this time. Her sorrow had become too big for me to handle alone. I wanted her back, not this creature who sipped tea as if it were poison. And I wanted to be able to live my own life. I wanted to go to Paris.

With determined steps, I walked across the room to the telephone that hung on the wall with its long cord dangling down toward the floor. I picked up the receiver. I would call 911. I didn't care what Mom would think or do. I couldn't save her.

My finger hesitated over the buttons. I didn't want strangers to take my mother away to the hospital like a criminal. And everyone in the Building there to watch them load her into the ambulance, like when Hunter had died.

My eyes wandered the list of emergency phone numbers taped to the wall beside the phone. Who else could help? Then I saw it. Doctor Singh. Our family doctor since I could remember. She was older than Mom. Her black hair had a touch of silver at the temples, and the skin around her eyes crinkled when she smiled.

The message service asked me if it was an emergency. I looked at Mom. She was staring into her cup, crying tears like hot tea. Lost to me again. She didn't even notice that I was in the room, talking on the phone about her.

"Yes. It's an emergency," I said.

Brad continued snoring from the next room.

* * *

I FINISHED CHOOSING MY ART CLASSES in the hospital waiting room before Dad even arrived. After that, it was easy to mail the letter.

Mom was in the hospital for days. Dad stayed with us at the apartment. Brad visited her once, and he told me that Dad went almost every day, but I couldn't make myself go.

I had betrayed her. I had turned her into the authorities. She would never forgive me.

After seven days, I couldn't put it off much longer. I had to see her. To tell her what I had done, where I was going in only two weeks. I had to tell her about Paris.

I didn't expect her to be different—I couldn't let myself hope. She'd had doctors before, but they'd never seemed to stick long enough to make any real change. At least, it had never stopped the night watches. Yet maybe this time would be different. Maybe this time I could get my mother back.

I went alone. They had her in the psych ward. I had to sign in with the nurse at the desk.

"Room 401. Down the hall to your left."

The hospital corridor smelled sour. My shoes tapped on the polished floor. The door to room 401 was open. Two beds. Mom on the one by the window. The window had bars on it.

My mother's eyes were red and swollen. Her hands trembled. Her voice was only a whisper.

"Allie. I'm so glad ..."

Mom propped herself up in the bed. Her pale blond hair was clean but it still hung limp against her face. She folded and unfolded her legs, not sure how to get settled.

"How are you, Mom?"

"I'm ... OK." She tried to smile at me. Her eyes watered. "I'm glad you came. I want to talk to you."

She didn't seem to remember that I had betrayed her.

"Me too." I dared to step closer.

"You first," she said.

"No, you."

She looked at her hands for help. I wobbled where I stood. Her fingers clutched and skated over each other.

When she looked up, I saw tears hovering on the bottom lid of each eye, anticipating the long journey down. She inhaled a jerky breath that caught me deep inside. My body became a stone statue. Cemented to the floor. Stiff with waiting for whatever was to come.

"I want you to know why I am like this. I want you to know what has been happening to me. For the last year, I've been remembering ... these things. I ... remember ... horrible ... things. Things that happened to me when I was a girl."

Tears began to find the way down her cheeks. I was still stone, but my stomach was beginning to feel sick. "What things?"

"Your Uncle Alex. He used to ..." She shook her head. "I can't," she paused then said all in a rush, "talk about it yet."

"Oh."

I got an unwanted memory of Uncle Alex. Family dinners—until we stopped going. A balding, large man with big hands. Uncle Alex had smoked a pipe and kept mints in his pocket. He had always hugged me a little too tight, a little too long. I remembered squirming desperately away.

My hands tightened into fists. Horrible images flashed into my mind. I imagined Uncle Alex's fat hands on my mother. Why was she telling me this? What had he done? I didn't know, but I could imagine the worst. I squeezed my eyes shut and pushed the images away.

"Just know that I'm going to try to sort myself out," Mom said, sounding stronger. "That I'm going to work through some things."

I opened my eyes. "OK." A warble crept into my voice as I reminded myself that I couldn't rescue her. I couldn't know if Mom was really going to get better this time. That was up to her, not me. I couldn't be her mother any more.

A nurse rolled a cart down the hallway, glancing in at us as she passed. Mom wiped her tears away.

"Mom, I have something to tell you, too."

"What?"

I stepped toward the bed. Leaned on it for support. "I've been accepted into that special arts program. A scholarship, so you don't have to pay. It's only for six months. Please, Mom. I want to go. Oh, I hope you say yes because I already chose my courses. Please, can I go?"

"Oh, Allie!" She began to cry all over again. "What you must have been through because of me. I'm so sorry." She wiped her eyes and reached for me. "I'm so proud of you."

She wasn't mad at me. She understood. "You mean I can go?"

She paused and her voice changed to a concerned mother's. "After I hear more about it."

I smiled at Mom in the hospital bed. She must be hurting, but I'd had a glimpse of who she used to be. Of how proud she was of me. Of how much she cared.

"Oh, Mom." I threw myself onto her. Wrapped arms around her in a melting hug.

A tear dripped warmth onto my cheek and slid down my neck. I squeezed her tighter. Her heart beat against mine. Her breath was in my ear. Her hand smoothed my hair.

"Tell me," she said when I finally pulled away.

"It's called Arts Abroad. Remember? I showed you the brochure in September." I crossed my legs and got comfortable on the end of her bed. "I'll be staying in a girls-only residence." I gave her a knowing smile. "But the art classes! Wait until you hear about them!"

Easy Target

Asim

Apt. 1005

THE PROBLEM WITH BEING THE OLDEST was that I had to baby-sit. Mother worked nights cleaning office towers downtown and Father sometimes worked later than expected at the hospital. Which left me stuck at home until he came. Yet that night was a big night for me. I was going out with my friends, and nothing would keep me from it.

Except for Father. He was late. Again. That was when my little brother Nassir—a five-year-old earthquake—decided that the bathwater belonged on the bathroom floor. My sister Fatima was no help in cleaning it up. Fatima was ten years old and mad that she wasn't in charge.

"You're the baby-sitter, Asim," she said without looking away from her book. Her long hair gleamed in the bright overhead light. Fatima had stopped wearing her *hijab* after a girl at her school had spit on her. A headscarf made her too much of a target. I knew how she felt.

Then I caught the baby, Rakia, pulling a box of noodles out of the kitchen cupboard and dumping it on the clean kitchen floor. She gurgled and tried to lift a noodle with one finger.

I sighed with frustration. Where was Father? If only I could leave the mess and dash out the door. Instead, I picked Rakia up so she wouldn't choke on a piece of hard noodle and tried to clean the mess with one hand. By the time Father walked through the door, the slow burn inside me was about to explode into fireworks.

I crunched over the spilled noodles, a dustpan in one hand and Rakia in the other. "You're late."

He was still wearing the loose clothing of an intern. In Egypt, he had been a doctor, but here he had to re-qualify. Father shot me a dark, stern look that said *respect your father.* I could only think that times had changed since he was a boy, running the market streets in Cairo.

I could hear Nassir hollering at Fatima down the hall, and she was giving it back to him double time.

"Silence," Father's voice was firm yet he did not yell.

The apartment became quiet and still. Fatima came running down the hall.

"Is there supper for me?" Father asked.

"I'll get it, Father." Fatima began to heat his meal in the microwave.

Now she helps, I thought, as I emptied the dustpan into the garbage.

Then I noticed the time. The kitchen clock showed that I was twenty minutes late already. Were my friends still waiting for me? Would they leave without me? I rushed to the room I shared with Nassir and dressed in black jeans, a new T-shirt, and a modern jacket. Western clothes. By then, Father had eaten and was preparing for his evening prayer.

"May I go now?" I asked, trying not to sound impatient.

"Are you not staying?"

"Don't you remember? I'm going out with friends ..."

"Oh." He laid out his prayer rug. "Yes."

I knew he wanted me to stay with him and I felt the pressure of guilt and obligation in my chest. I wished he understood how I wanted a different life from his. I wanted to fit in with my friends—to belong to the culture that I had grown up in. I stood, waiting.

"The keys are in the hall," Father said, his eyes sharp on me.

"OK."

I peeled Rakia out of my arms and handed her to Fatima, her nose in her book again. Rakia made a face and reached her arms out for me.

"Where did you leave it?" I called to Father.

"In the outside parking lot."

I made a dash for the door before Rakia began to wail. I was kind of a favorite of hers because I played a mean game of peek-a-boo.

I burst out of the apartment into the hallway, right into a large man with big ears and a red nose.

"Watch where you're going, you little A-rab." He grabbed my arm. Beside him stood a tiny girl with long messy blond hair.

I gasped. Not again. Not like those bullies at school. When would these people leave me alone? "Go home terrorist!" the bullies had called to me outside after school. Between classes, they bumped me in the hall and gave me the finger. It was the hatred in their eyes that scared me most.

"So sorry." I had learned not to talk back. I tried to back away but the man held my arm fast.

His face was twisted in anger. "We never asked you A-rabs to come here. Why don't you go back where you came from?" He squeezed my arm until I gritted my teeth.

Let me go, I thought. Just let me go.

"Sorry." I whispered through the pain.

"Yeah, you should be sorry. Now get outta here." He released my arm with a push that sent me sprawling.

"Ha, ha, ha," he laughed, then stepped over me and walked away. The little girl watched me with big frightened eyes, like I was some kind of monster.

I know who the monster is, I thought, clenching my fists. Yet I didn't dare return the attack. Father had told me enough times that violence was not the way to solve problems.

My ears were still echoing with the man's laughter when I left the Building, so the quiet of the city night was a relief. There was only the sound of cars, the wind pushing brown leaves around, and some kids yelling in the far distance.

I dodged between the two shopping carts abandoned near Father's rusted gray mini-van. As I unlocked the door, I checked my reflection in the side window. I had worn clothes that I thought would help me fit in, but I was still a target. Thick black eyebrows, brown eyes, a straight nose, brown skin. What did it matter how I looked or where my family came from? I'd lived here for as long as I could remember. When would I belong?

I cranked the van's engine a little too long and it protested. The radio whined with a song from Father's Arab station. I twirled the dial until I found a new dance tune, then swung the van out of the driveway, bopping my head in time to the beat. I began to relax and enjoy myself.

Few cars were out—as if it were the middle of the night. The streetlights flashed a rhythm of light and dark on the dashboard. Minutes later I parked the van neatly against the curb opposite the bank. It was right across from the subway stop, so I was glad to find a place to park. Just a quick trip in for some money and I'd be off. I didn't have a part-time job, but at least Father gave me money occasionally in return for "fulfilling my family responsibilities."

On the way in, I passed a skinny, pale woman and some kids, but not many others were around. The wind was too cold. It sliced through my jacket and chilled me.

I slid my card through the scanner to open the door. In front of the bank machine, I couldn't decide how much money to take out. We were going to meet at a fast-food place then go to an all-ages dance club. I squirmed around, trying to decide how much to withdraw. Until a woman behind me said, "Hurry up, kid."

I jumped at the sound of her voice. The woman was wearing a long, dirty, burgundy coat, and she was breathing in deep noisy gulps of air. Was she a weirdo or just a late-night banker? I decided to treat myself generously, grabbed my money, and headed for the door.

On my way back to the van, I started to think about my friends. I'd just met them at school, although they'd been friends for a while. Saied, who was slick and had a way with the girls. Travis, who would belly flop into any sign of trouble, then scream at us to get him out. And Raz, who could flip a quarter off the table and catch it in his teeth. I was wishing I could go out every night, like my friends did, so I hardly heard the small voice.

"Hey there!" a girl's voice called.

Who had spoken? I glanced at the woman and kids. They were huddled against the wall next to the darkened windows of the dentist's office. A baby was sleeping in a stroller beside two young girls with worried eyes. The woman—their mother probably—looked like somebody had pulled her plug and drained the life out of her.

"Did you say something?" I asked, although I didn't want to get involved.

"Yeah," began the oldest girl. She had long blond hair like the girl in the Building but she wasn't scared of me. "Uh, sorry to ask you but ..." She spoke in hesitant, faltering bursts. "We, uh, took the bus and the subway from the other side of the city because we heard that the Church of Saint Martin had a food bank." The girl gestured down the street to where the church was. I passed it every day on the way to school.

"But when we got there," she continued, "it was closed. Please, do you have some money so we can get home on the subway?"

I stood there, staring at them. The girl pleaded with her eyes. The mother, who wore a thin green jacket over tight purple pants, started weeping with her head hung down to hide her face. The younger girl was gripping her mother's arm as if she were trying to hold her up. As I stared at her, the mother's sobs grew louder.

I looked at the baby bundled in a grubby blanket. Rakia would be snug inside our apartment, gulping back her last bottle in a warm crib with more toys than bed.

Then the baby woke up and started crying a waterfall. He looked a bit older than Rakia, but he wasn't so chubby. His howling was bothering me. I wanted him to stop.

My brain danced with thoughts. They had no food. Their clothes were so worn. They needed to get home. Yet these were the kind of people who hassled me all the time. Like the boys at school. Like the rough man in the hallway. Like the girl who had spit on my sister. These were the people I had learned to avoid. Should I help them now? What would Father do?

I took one of the scrunched twenty-dollar bills out of my pocket. It was either that or a few coins. I tried to put the money into the mother's hand, but she was sobbing so much that she didn't see me. I offered the money to the older girl.

"Here you go."

At the same moment I handed over the money, the baby stopped crying. It was like he knew he was taken care of now.

"Thanks!" The girl's voice gushed over me with a sweetness that was for real. The mother, seeing the money, nodded her thanks through a blanket of tears.

"OK," I mumbled.

I walked dumbly across the street toward Father's van and opened the driver's door. The inside of the van was so worn that the rug was scruffy and frayed. Then the question hit me like a kick to the head—why had they come all that way without any money to get home? Had I been conned? Did the mother teach her kids the right way to look and just what to say to fool people out of their money? Were they laughing now and calling me a stupid A-rab?

I was an easy target. My friends loved telling me lies that were so tall and mixed with the truth that I swallowed them whole. I fell for it every time. It was a running joke with them. I always felt foolish afterward, hating them for teasing me. Like the time that Saied convinced me that the police had arrested Travis for disturbing the peace. They hadn't, of course, but my friends had a good laugh. And now, had I been tricked again?

I got into the van and watched the family trundle down the sidewalk. They had just realized how much money I had given them. A windfall for them. A spot of bad luck turned good. They saw me tracking them with my eyes, so the whole family stood waving and shouting at me from the edge of the sidewalk.

"Thank you. Thank you." Their eyes shone with relief, and they were grateful.

Grateful for twenty dollars. It was enough money to do something. Maybe a subway ride home and a few meals, if they worked the money right. What was twenty dollars to me? I could go back to the money machine for more.

Then I remembered how, every year, Father made me give some of my money away. "Charity is required of every Muslim," he would say. I had always resented Father for making me give *zakat*, and I had never gotten the point—until now.

As I watched the family head for the subway—still waving at me—I should have been proud. After all, I had performed an act of charity. Yet I could offer so much more. Maybe if I had volunteered to baby-sit. Or asked Mother to send them Rakia's old clothes.

The family was about to fade into the night—into the noise and traffic of the city. The food I was about to eat would be a real feast to them. I had to do something.

I whirled the van around to the other side of the street until I was alongside them. Switched into park, opened the driver's side window, and stuck my head out.

"Do you want a ride home?" I said, then I wished I hadn't. What if they thought I was trying to hurt them? What if they looked at me as if I were a terrorist? I held my breath.

The older girl glanced from me to her mother. The mother wiped one eye clear of tears.

I had to make them understand who I was. I had to make them see that I was not a threat. Father had told me that my name meant "protector." Asim, the protector. Not a terrorist. Not a victim. I leaped out and slid open the side door.

"I've even got a car seat for the baby." I showed them. "It's my sister's."

The mother smiled through her tears. The girl spoke for her. "Thank you."

"Hop in," I said.

It was only one night. My friends could wait.

The Many Faces of Men, Boys, and Pigs

Cori

Apt. 111

AT BREAKFAST, MY MOTHER ANGRILY COOKED eggs for my father. "What am I, the family slave?" she asked.

Her back was straight and stiff, and she was poking at the eggs with sharp jabs of the spatula. Considering I just set the table and got my own breakfast, I didn't agree with her. Yet she was hissing like a teakettle, so I said nothing.

"Cori," she said. "Remember never to become a servant in your own home. A slave to one man's desires." Then she announced in a loud voice, "Men are pigs. Never forget that."

This was what my mother had to teach me—that all men were pigs and all women had to somehow survive them.

I looked at my father. He had a small coffee stain on the front of his dress shirt. His easy brown eyes swallowed me whole.

"What did I do?" His eyes almost made me sorry for him, but he didn't move to help. Instead, he unfolded the newspaper and scanned the front page.

Mom slammed the eggs down in front of him. Dad ate in big gulps before he rushed out the door to work, with

Mom pulling on her coat right behind him. They raced to see who could get out of the apartment first.

From behind the smudged glass doors of our first-floor walkout, I watched them zoom out of the underground and away with squealing tires and burning rubber. Dad drives a dented red sports car with two seats. When he gives me a ride I have to squeeze between old newspapers and empty coffee cups. Mom's car is a faded green station wagon with fake wood on the outside, but it is always spotless inside.

* * *

THE FIRST TIME A BOY TOUCHED ME in that sort of way was a few weeks later in media studies class, after Mr. Rollo had turned out the lights and put on a show. We sat at round tables in media class, with four to a table. At my table was Cheryl the boring non-stop talker, Patrick the too-tall geek boy, and Ron the beautiful brown-skinned wonder.

At first, I couldn't figure out what was tickling my leg. Then I realized that Ron was reaching his foot under the table and oh-so-gently stroking my calf. I didn't know whether to move away. Was this an accident? Was he trying to scratch an itchy toe against the table leg? I looked into beautiful Ron's face, and he smiled a sweet smile without showing his teeth. Perfect. The soft stroke of his toe shot fire through me. I fell in love.

After that, every time Mr. Rollo turned out the lights for a show I longed for Ron's touch, and every time, Ron reached under the table toward me. We didn't talk, unless we were assigned a group project. It was as if that one probing toe and an accepting calf said it all.

Yet all was not right. I started to have dreams at night about Ron. Not dreams of bodies dripping desire. I dreamed that Ron was trying to sneak a peek at me while I was in my bedroom, changing my clothes. I pulled down the blind, but he was still outside my window, trying to peer through any tiny crack he could find. In my dream, I hid in the closet to dress, then sneaked over to the window and snapped up the blind, surprising him. What I found wasn't Ron, but a plump, pink pig with deep chocolate eyes like Ron's. He snuffled his snout at me then ran away. I woke up. I hate living on the first floor. When we moved to the Building, I told my parents not to take an apartment on the first floor. Even when Petra got kidnapped, they wouldn't listen. They just had to have that first-floor walkout.

In media class, our tablemates, Cheryl and Patrick, couldn't help but watch our silent talk. Patrick surprised me with the pig-side of his nature on the way into class one day, although I should have expected it.

"Getting it on with Ron?" he asked.

Flustered, and caught in the act, I sneered at him in a way I hoped was sophisticated. "You're such a pig, Patrick."

He chuckled, then folded his long body into his chair and under the table. As I took my seat across from Ron, I could feel Patrick's heavy-lidded eyes on Ron and me.

When the lights dimmed, I moved my legs far away where Ron couldn't reach. Ron shot me puzzled, hurt looks. *Come back to me?* his eyes said.

In the hall after class, Cheryl battered me with words without even taking a breath. "So, are you and Ron an item? Everyone is talking about it and I just want to know first-hand what is going on. Has he asked you to be his girlfriend? Are you going steady? Have you slept with him yet? You know, Jackie Markham went out with him last year for one month. She won't talk to him now, and she won't say why. I figure that he must have done something really bad. What do you think he did? Has he done anything to you?"

Other people's romances excited Cheryl, if you could call a toe probe a romance. She'd never been out on a date or anything. No one could stand her endless gab.

"Ron?" I tried to act surprised, and I talked loud enough for him to hear. "Why would I go out with Ron?"

As soon as I said the words, I desperately wanted to go out with him. My leg longed for his touch. At night, my dreams were no longer about disturbed pigs. Instead, I dreamed fairy-tale romances of lifelong love. I woke hopeless, though, sure that I had lost my chance with Ron.

In the next media class, I again offered him my leg when the lights dimmed. I scrunched my eyes and waited for his caress.

Nothing. Nothing. Nothing. Damn it, nothing.

He made me wait until almost the end, when Mr. Rollo was heading for the light switch. I was ready to cry, so it was with relief and astonishment that I felt the soft lick of his toe.

I decided to make a move for Ron. I told Cheryl I liked him, and she did the rest. She told Ron's best friend Steve about it, and Steve told Ron. At least, that's how I guessed it happened, because Steve found me just before drama class.

"So I hear you like Ron."

He was the messenger so I couldn't tell him to mind his own business. I shrugged. "I might."

Steve the messenger said, "Well, Ron says he'll go out with you if you'll sleep with him."

Just like that. Like it was a simple deal to make.

I skipped drama class, and cried in the bathroom instead. I decided men really were pigs. My mother was right.

* * *

I MANAGED TO STOP CRYING LONG ENOUGH to walk to my locker, shove my books into my backpack, and head for the exit. Two classes to go, but I'd rather get caught skipping than stay in the same building as Ron. I pounded down the stairs, stomping out Steve's words with each step. I imagined the metal door was beautiful Ron's face, and I kicked it open with the bottom of my high-heeled boot.

I was never so glad to see the Building; all I wanted was the safety of my own apartment. By the time I got to my door, I couldn't see past the tears to slide the key into the lock. I wiped my eyes furiously. Ron the pig couldn't have this much control over me. Finally, I got the door unlocked and pushed it open with my shoulder. On the other side of the door I was surprised to find my mother with enough tears to match my own.

"What happened, Cori? Oh, baby, are you OK?" My mother tried to wipe the sorrow from my face with her own tear-stained fingers. She didn't even ask if I was skipping school.

I pulled away. "What happened to you?" We stared at one another with puffy, red eyes—the color of love.

Mom was the first to turn away. "It's your father," she said with a slump of her narrow shoulders. "I met him for lunch. He threatened to move out. He's tired of the fights."

I noticed her auburn hair then, cut in short feathery strands close to her face. Her almond skin and fine bones. Her smart crimson business suit. She was a tidy package. I also saw myself in her. Small weak bones, frail flesh, and red hair the color of heartbreak. A squawk like a strangled chicken escaped from my throat, and more salt water beat a path down my cheeks.

My mother forgot to ask about my tears—she was too caught up in her own. She headed for the bathroom to tidy herself up, and I ran to my bed to share my heartache with my pillow.

I cried into my blankets. I cried to Allie, my best friend in the Building. I yelled at my father for no reason. He grounded me for a month, but I had nowhere to go.

* * *

I HAD FALLEN FOR RON IN LESS THAN A SECOND, but it took me months to pull myself out of the raw, bleeding place he'd driven me to. Allie was gone by then. She had abandoned me for some art school in Paris. Of all people, it was Cheryl I saw first when I raised my head out of the mud—a spring flower ready to bloom.

I wasn't ready to get bitten again by that crazy love bug that hunted all animals in the spring. My plan was to learn to mingle. Cheryl was the perfect partner. She would talk for me.

Not many from our school hung with Cheryl, so she had fallen in with her cousin's friends from a private school further downtown. A rich crowd—with cars, cool clothes, and cash. They never had dates—just gangs going out together.

Cheryl and I took the subway to her cousin Sylvia's neighborhood. I wouldn't want stuck-up Sylvia and her friends to pick me up at the Building. We drove to a new all-ages dance club. It took two cars to hold us all. Cheryl and I were squeezed into the back with Mike, the rich boy who had everything. In the front seat, Sylvia snuggled beside her boyfriend Bryce, who was driving his father's BMW. The rest were in Serina's Jetta—her parents had bought it for her three weeks ago.

Mike made me forget my promise to myself not to fall in love. He had a soft voice, loose, dark curls, and a lean, hard body.

Sylvia was whispering sweet nothings into Bryce's ear. She giggled as he groped her with one hand, the other gripping the wheel. Cheryl was talking, of course.

"I've heard about this club. My cousin goes there all the time. It's a strange name for a club, don't you think? The Earwig. Kind of gross. Makes me think of bugs, not music. I'll be checking my drink for any crunchy bits, that's for sure. It will be so dark that we won't be able to see any little creatures that may be crawling around on the floor. I think they should change the name. Don't you?"

Cheryl managed to keep it up all the way to the club. She talked more when she was nervous. Mike and I spoke without words. Our legs touched and once his hand caressed mine.

At the club, the speakers blasted out dance tunes so loud my chest pounded the beat. I couldn't help but move to the rhythm. The dance floor was a mass of people. Most couples didn't dance together, except for the rare slow song when they paused long enough to hang onto each other and catch their breath.

I was drawn to this fast world. I had no time for Ron or his footsy games. I danced alone, song after song, burning off the pain, the sorrow, and the anger of Ron. I was caught in a spinning, dizzying zone. Until I could dance no longer. I rested as far from the booming music as I could get.

Mike found me. "I saw you dancing." He nodded his approval and sat beside me on the small ledge that was once a windowsill—before they bricked in the window. His leg touched mine.

My face heated up. I forgot that others would be watching my dance, but I was flattered by Mike's attention.

We could barely hear to talk. We leaned close together, cheek to cheek, lips brushing each other's ears. I could smell his cologne, feel his warmth. Yet I didn't look at his face. We would be close enough to kiss.

I learned that Mike was a rich boy who didn't have everything. He was sad. He told me about his father. How he was a busy lawyer and a politician. How he never had time for Mike. Mike was lonely. No one understood him.

I pressed against Mike to comfort him. I wanted to sweep my lips over his, but his friends appeared. Cheryl, too.

"Ready to split?" asked Bryce as Sylvia nuzzled against him in the way that I wanted to nuzzle Mike.

It was not a question. Bryce was the driver. He said when it was time to go. He dropped Cheryl and me off at the subway. Cheryl was jabbering, but I must have passed the test because Mike asked me to come to a party with his friends. We would go to someone's farmhouse-cottage northwest of the city. We would stay overnight.

Mike whispered in my ear, "See you next Saturday?"

I nodded. We had a date, sort of. Cheryl and the others would come, too.

What Mom and Dad didn't know wouldn't hurt them. Mom dropped me in front of Cheryl's house for a sleepover—Cheryl's parents let her get away with more. With our overnight bags, we walked to the bus stop in the rain. We took the subway downtown to Mike's neighborhood. Bundled into a car with booze and Mike's friends, we drove for two hours to the party.

"Come on," said Mike to me. "Let's find someplace quiet."

The party was happening in the kitchen, but, after a few drinks, we went to a bedroom.

I kissed Mike, though he had more than a kiss on his mind. He pushed me down onto the bed and tried to reach inside my clothes.

"Come on, Cori. Let's do it." He nibbled my neck.

I didn't want to do it with him. I didn't want to do it with anyone yet.

"No. Stop."

"You're a wild girl. You sure dance like one." He breathed into my ear.

He was a poor rich boy. Sensitive, yet sexy.

"No." I pushed him hard—off me, off the bed. A tumble of clothes and skin bumped the floor.

"Hey!" he yelled.

But he stopped. It could have been worse. He pulled on his shirt and left me alone.

I didn't see him for the rest of the night. Instead, I locked the door and cried. Later, I tried to sleep away my disappointment, but nightmares of Ron and Mike haunted me.

In the morning, Bryce drove us to Cheryl's. Me on one side of the backseat and Mike on the other. Cheryl sat between us, with Mike's arm around her shoulder. They whispered together the whole way home.

* * *

I SWORE OFF ROMANCE FOR MONTHS, but not for good. I was too weak to resist forever.

My father hadn't moved out, but he walked around the apartment with heavy footsteps and eyes that smoldered. Until he missed supper one night. More than supper, actually. He didn't come home until morning. I could hear the fight from my room.

"You smell like perfume!" my mother yelled. "Who do you think you're fooling?"

My father said that he was sorry. That it wouldn't happen again.

My mother wouldn't talk to him, and she wouldn't make him breakfast anymore. Dad avoided looking at her or me.

"What should I do?" my mother asked me when we were alone, like I was some kind of expert on love. "Maybe I should leave him."

She didn't say what would happen to me if she left. And she didn't leave. She scrubbed the kitchen instead. And the bathroom, the living room, the bedrooms. Our apartment was spotless. Without a blemish.

"Men are evil, stupid, worthless pigs. Don't be a victim, Cori." My mother's words rang in my ears.

I agreed.

* * *

SCHOOL DIDN'T KEEP ME BUSY ENOUGH to avoid Cheryl and Ron, and I refused to clean with my mother. So I started a strict exercise routine. Jogged for an hour before school each morning, never missed a high-impact aerobics class at the community center, and ate like a workhorse in between.

I promised myself I wouldn't become one of those stupid women who believed in love. I refused to dream at night. Yet Paul battered my defenses with kindness. I met him at the gym. Paul the caveman. Blond, with a barrel chest, and muscle-man arms. He worked in a warehouse, lifting boxes. I was unprepared for his kindness.

For four months, he asked me out after each aerobics class—three times a week. At first, I didn't even answer him, but he persisted. So I pushed him away with words, although I did notice his strong legs and cute butt as he jumped around trying to keep up with the instructor's routine.

Finally, I agreed to one date, just to get rid of him. One date became two, then three, and then we fell into an easy dating pattern that stretched into eight months. I guess we were a couple, although I never meant for it to happen. I became used to having Paul around. I expected him to be with me.

Until one night in the weight room, when I was watching Paul beat his own record with the free weights.

"Yes!" he yelled after he lowered the bar back into the rack. Walker, who was almost as big as Paul, patted him on the back as Paul wiped down the bench for him.

Paul was nice, but sometimes he got on my nerves. He kissed me slowly and he didn't push for more. He never so much as glanced at another girl. He knew he couldn't, or I'd leave him. Still, he grunted when he dropped the barbell, his sweat had a moldy smell, and he swallowed his food in big bites without chewing. I couldn't keep quiet.

"What a man," I said so he could hear. "He can lift heavy weights. Grunt for me, caveman."

A few people laughed with me. Gemma the priss just raised one eyebrow at me. Paul said nothing. Just took it all in. He knew I was hurting. I'd told him about Ron and Mike. And Dad.

I knew I was wrong, but something in me couldn't stop. Men deserved it, didn't they? They were all pigs. "You know how Paul counts how much weight he's lifted? By stomping on the floor!" I pounded the floor like a dumb mule. "One, two, three, ... uh ... seventeen?"

Walker and some of the other guys and girls were gathering around. They sniggered and howled. Gemma moved away, shaking her head.

"Ever see a monkey trying to write his name? You haven't seen Paul signing a check." Paul hadn't finished grade 10. I liked to tease him about that.

Paul grabbed his towel and flung it over one shoulder. "I'm hitting the showers."

I opened my mouth to hurl one last gem but something about Paul's sloping shoulders, his hand rubbing one eye, stopped me.

* * *

ON THE WAY HOME, PAUL PULLED THE CAR to a stop on the side of the road. He switched off the radio—a crooning song of a lover's deceit.

"Hey, I'm listening to that."

"I've got something to say," he mumbled into his lap.

"Hold it, everyone," I called to the imaginary crowd. "Paul has something to say."

His face flushed. Then he said, "I can't see you anymore, Cori."

I was shocked. Dumbfounded. *Paul* was dumping *me*?

"This is a joke," I began, reaching for his hand. "You can't ..."

"No joke." He pulled back his hand and clenched the steering wheel. "It's not that I don't like you. I do. But ..."

He gripped the wheel tighter. "You're a cruel bitch sometimes."

What was he talking about? I wasn't a bitch. The blood drained from my body until my head grew dizzy. My new firm muscles tightened around me.

"No!" The word roared from my mouth. This couldn't be happening. Ron and Mike had only wanted me if I would sleep with them, but Paul was supposed to be different. He was supposed to want me and respect me no matter what.

"No use talking about it." Paul put the car in drive and stared through the windshield. His chin was rigid but his eyes looked misty from the side. "I've made up my mind." Then he added more softly, "I'll take you home."

I couldn't see Paul for the tears.

I shut my eyes to force them back. The car swayed around corners. How could Paul do this to me? I wasn't a bitch. He provoked me. Didn't he?

Ten minutes later, the car pulled to a stop. I opened my eyes to the Building. Paul's headlights shone on the white-brick wall to the underground. I watched the shadows of two people turning the corner of the Building. The lights in the lobby glowed a jaundiced yellow through the glass doors.

"Goodbye, Cori."

I wiped my hands across my eyes to clear the tears. I wanted to fling myself over the parking brake at Paul. Prove to him somehow that he was wrong. That he did want me. Yet an invisible barrier had sprung up between us. Maybe it had always been there. Ron, Mike, and even Dad hovering between us like a ghostly wall.

"Paul?"

I wanted to tell him how I wasn't a bitch. How I was hurting from so many injustices.

He flinched as if I were about to throw something at him. "Don't make this any harder, Cori."

I hated how he said my name. Cori. With a too-hard C and an extra-long O. He had never said it that way before.

"I just wanted to say goodbye." I sniffled, waiting for him to change his mind.

He didn't.

I got out of the car and shut the door. Through the window, I caught a glimpse of his face from the side. One man's face. Square chin. Shaved head. Nose twice broken in hockey. Freckled cheeks.

I stared at him, remembering how Paul smelled like earth after a spring rain. How his lips tasted like butter. How he dreamed of a business of his own one day—landscaping. He wanted to make flowers grow.

Paul pulled away from me then. His car circled the drive and turned onto the street, his red taillights winking goodbye.

Hot tears raced down my cheeks, and I heard the echo of my mother's voice. *Men are pigs. Never forget that.* Maybe some were. But not Paul. The trouble was, Paul was gone.

Off the Couch

Roger

Apt. 615

MOM ALWAYS CALLED ME LAZY, but I would do anything for a pepperoni pizza with double cheese and anchovies, a late-night kung-fu show, or eggs. Sixteen white eggs. Chicken eggs, I guessed.

Mom, Kate and I were on the couch watching TV when Dad showed up without warning. He smelled like cigarettes. Snowflakes were melting into his hair. I couldn't remember when I last saw him. Maybe it was spring.

"Daddy?" asked Kate as if she wasn't sure who he was.

"Hey, baby!" Dad set an incubator down on the coffee table beside me. "There you go, Roger! The eggs are cold now. Just plug it in and you're ready to go."

The incubator was shaped like a flying saucer with a clear plastic dome. As large as the whole tabletop, it could have been a prop in a cheap outer-space show.

"For me?" I asked, leaning sideways to look at it. Dad had probably won it in a card game and didn't know how else to get rid of it.

"Sure is!" He slapped the side of the incubator and I cringed, imagining the eggs cracking and the yolks spilling out.

"What does he need that for?" Mom stood to face him. Her eyes had that cold mean stare. Her neck muscles popped out in solid cords.

I sunk back into the couch. Kate cuddled closer to me, yanking nervously on one of the tight little braids Mom had worked into her hair.

Dad's eye darted away from Mom. "The boy's seventeenth birthday ought to be special. I'm just trying to make something of it."

I was going to say that he'd missed my birthday. That it was last month. But Mom interrupted.

"Make something of your support payments, why don't you? We need them more than a stupid incubator." Her voice pierced like a sliver.

Dad wrung his gloves in his hands. He backed out of the apartment. I knew how he felt.

"Don't forget those payments," Mom yelled down the hall at him.

"Bye-bye, Daddy," Kate whispered.

I watched Mom march back in. The TV droned out an infomercial for a new shampoo. With her hands on her hips, Mom stared at the incubator.

"I guess it's scrambled eggs for supper," she said with a sigh.

"No."

I hauled myself up off the couch and stood in front of the incubator with my arms out beside me. My big stomach probably blocked it all.

"Oh, come on, Roger."

Kate came to stand with me, her thumb in her mouth and her blanket trailing behind her.

"I want to see the eggs," she said, without removing her thumb.

"Oh, save me, sweet angels." My mother shook her head and walked away. I heard her opening the fridge and slamming food on the counter.

I carried the incubator to my room and set it on the floor. Kate followed me. I plugged in the incubator. The light glowed yellow and warmed my hands through the plastic. Someone had drawn a tiny X in pencil on each egg. Why?

I watched until one moved. At least I thought it moved.

* * *

MOM DIDN'T MENTION THE EGGS AGAIN. Until she caught Kate and me watching a nature program two days later. A special on creatures that laid eggs. I didn't know I was supposed to turn the eggs.

Mom came in from her Saturday lunch shift at the restaurant. She flung her brown tweed coat onto a kitchen chair. When she saw, on the TV, the fat mother hen settling on her eggs, Mom switched to the news.

"Don't think you're keeping those things if they hatch. You'd better find a place for them or it's straight down the garbage chute they go."

Beside me on the couch, Kate sobbed and pulled her blanket over her head. Mom settled into a chair with the converter.

I put my arm around Kate. She peeked through the holes in her blanket.

"I'll take care of it," I said.

We watched the news. I began to wonder what was inside the eggs. They were the size and shape of eggs from the store, but were they chicken eggs? Or maybe duck? Or even snake? If I knew where Dad was living, I could ask him.

* * *

"YOU NEED A LIBRARY CARD to take out books."

The librarian looked over the desk at me with a forgiving smile. Three books were piled between us on the counter. *From Egg to Chicken. Critters That Hatch. Inside an Egg.*

"Oh," I said. I should have known that.

The line-up of people behind me leaned in to listen. I wished I could have shrunk. What was the point of being big if it only made me a better target?

"I went to a library once with Mrs. C." Kate beamed at the librarian over the edge of the counter. "She got a movie about a girl mouse. Do you have that movie here?"

The librarian shook her head and slid a paper over to me. "You need to fill out this form."

"OK."

She made the whole line-up wait while she helped me with the form. I could hear the impatient shuffling and sighing behind me, but I got a library card and the three books.

Kate liked the pictures. We read them on the bus on the way back to the Building.

"Look, Roger! Lots of baby chicks all together! And a mommy one. She's sitting on her eggs, isn't she, Roger? Here's an egg cracking. Here's a just-born chick. It's all wet. Why is it all wet, Roger? Oh, I like this fluffy one, don't you?"

I was squeezed into a corner seat with Kate beside me. She held the book right up to my face so I couldn't see anything.

"Cute," I said.

Flynn and Tony were hanging outside the Building when we arrived.

"Roger has eggs." Kate bounced up and down on her heels. "He's going to make them hatch. Aren't you, Roger?"

"I guess."

Flynn hooted. "Welcome to the farm!" He pushed open one of the double doors for us—the lock was busted again so we didn't need a key.

Tony leaned against the other door and grinned wickedly. "Wouldn't want the super to hear about those eggs."

He glanced over at the super, Mag Jennings, slouched in her lawn chair outside her main-floor apartment. She was puffing on a cigarette and squinting over at us.

"Guess not." I pushed Kate inside before she could say anything else.

* * *

THAT NIGHT, MOM AND KATE WATCHED TV while I lay on my bed and read my library books. The bed was softer than the couch, and I propped my head up with a pillow. I didn't even miss my shows.

From the books, I learned what the X was for. Someone had marked the eggs for turning. Maybe it was Dad. Maybe he had done something right for a change.

I had to turn the eggs three times a day, just like a mama would. The eggs had tiny bumps all over them. When I turned them over the first time, I saw an O in pencil on the other side. X O X. Every day. O X O. Like the kisses and hugs on my birthday card from Mom. Kate noticed the O's, too.

"Can I color on them, too?" she asked.

"No coloring." I made her promise.

But she insisted on turning them. I didn't know how else to turn them while I was at school. So I turned them when I woke up and when I went to bed, and Kate turned them when I was at school. I told her to wash her hands before she turned the eggs, but I couldn't tell if she did. And I told her not to shake them.

At school I wondered about my eggs all the time. Most days, I did the least amount of work possible and avoided anyone who might want to push me around. Not that many did, because of my size, but a few who suspected that I was soft sometimes came after me. Like Josh, a basketball player with a big nose. Maybe he was trying to make up for the size of his honker, but he liked to pester me as I thumped down the hall.

"Hey, Black Jumbo, what's doing?" Josh bounded along beside me.

I could have pressed Josh away from me with one hand, but I didn't.

"Leave him alone." It was Jennifer, from the Building. I thought she was after Tony but she was draped over Josh right then.

Jennifer left off pawing Josh to link arms with me. "He doesn't know anything about race relations," she confided to me. Josh turned red in the face.

I shook Jennifer off. Why didn't everyone just leave me alone?

By day four, I knew just what to do with my eggs. I marked on my wall calendar each day that had passed with a big X. I kept the water pan in the incubator full of water. I kept the temperature set for chicken eggs just because I didn't know what else to do. Would Dad have given me snake eggs? The duck eggs in the book looked bigger than my eggs. So I guessed they were chicken eggs.

I now knew that chicken eggs took 21 days to hatch and duck eggs took longer. I didn't think I could hatch any eggs, but I had to try. I couldn't just let them die.

On the night of day seven, while I was turning them, I noticed a crack in one egg, and it wasn't hatching early. At first I thought it was a hair. The egg lay, like the others, with its bigger round end higher than the pointy end. Then I saw how the crack ran from the big end to the X in the middle and disappeared underneath.

Kate was already in bed. Mom had the TV blasting on some stupid sitcom. I found two eggs with cracks. They were ruined. Dead. Never to be hatched. It must have been Kate.

I thought that maybe I shouldn't let Kate touch them anymore. She might love them to death. Yet she cared about them almost as much as I did, and I couldn't stand her tears. What could I do?

I took the cracked eggs out of the incubator. They were small and white in my big brown hands. I remembered reading in one of the library books that only about half of all fertilized eggs hatch. With Kate around, I would be lucky to hatch any.

Mom looked up at me when I shuffled down the hall, an egg in each hand. She narrowed her eyes at the eggs. I waited for her to say something mean, but she just turned back to her show. Good thing she kept quiet. I might have thrown one at her.

I dropped the eggs down the garbage chute.

* * *

I STOPPED TURNING THE EGGS near the end because the book said to. It said that the chicks, if they were chicks, would be getting ready to hatch and not to disturb them. So I didn't.

Day nineteen passed with no hatching. And day twenty. And day twenty-one. I checked my calendar to see if I had counted wrong. I hadn't.

Then, on day twenty-two, Tony cornered me in the washroom at school.

"I heard you were moving in on Jennifer." He backed me into a corner, puffing out his chest like he meant to do me harm.

I shook my head. He only came up to my chin but I still didn't want to hurt him.

"Josh saw you in the parking lot with her. What do you say to that? You denying it?"

"You've got the wrong guy," I said. "Talk to Josh." Then I pushed past him and headed home. I had enough to worry about with my eggs. I didn't need his problems on me, too.

When I got home, Kate met me at the apartment door. She was bouncing on her toes.

"Roger, there's a crack in one egg." She pulled at my coat.

I remembered the two cracked eggs banging down the garbage chute. If she had cracked another one, I wouldn't be able to trust her with my eggs any more.

I raced down the hall to my room without even taking off my backpack. We passed Mom in the bathroom. The door was open a sliver and I could see her in her waitress uniform, trying to straighten her hair.

In my room, Kate pointed. "Look!" Her eyes were shining black jewels and her cheeks burned deep burgundy.

I looked. One egg had a hole in it. Not a crack like before, but a hole.

I felt my face heat up and I was about to set into Kate when I saw the egg move. Then a tiny point—maybe a beak—tapped a larger hole in the egg.

My eggs were hatching! They really were hatching! I couldn't believe it.

I could see another egg wiggling. Not like when I first got my eggs and I thought I saw one move. I mean, really rocking.

"Listen." Kate tucked her hand behind her ear and leaned over my eggs.

I turned one ear to them and heard a faint "peep."

Not snakes. Not lizards. Must be chickens. Baby chickens.

I smiled so wide my face felt as if it would split in two. If this was being a farmer, I liked it.

Mom came in after a while. She didn't say anything, but she watched for a long time. She watched with us as that one little chick cracked a line around the middle of the egg. I remembered that chicks have a small bump near the end of their beaks that they use to break out of their shells. Two other eggs were wiggling, and a hole appeared in a fourth egg. But that first chick was still way ahead.

It would stop for a while and I would think, don't stop. Keep going. You can do it.

Kate spoke in a whisper-song the whole time, "Come on out, little chickie. Come on."

After about two hours, my legs were cramped from kneeling on the floor. We were all crammed around that tiny incubator, although Kate would run around in excited circles every now and then. By then my chick had made a crack around the whole egg, but it took another half an hour for it to push one end of the egg off.

My first chick had hatched. Wet yellow feathers and a scrawny body. Too small to be alive. The chick was weak. It flopped down only half out of its shell to rest. I wanted to hold it, but I let it be.

"Angels above!" Mom whispered. She gripped my arm with a warm squeeze. I noticed that she was late for work. I guess my eggs weren't so bad after all.

Mom left soon after that. Kate and I watched three more chicks working to crack their eggs. I had to wonder how they knew just what to do. They all hatched the same way without any help from anyone.

In a few hours, two more chicks had hatched. Their feathers were beginning to dry, soft and fluffy yellow. Kate and I took turns holding them. They smelled like spring. I rubbed their feathers against my cheek.

Back in the incubator, my chicks were beginning to walk, but they were wobbly. They hopped about on their big-clawed feet and pecked at everything within reach.

The fourth chick had cracked a line around its egg but it couldn't seem to get out. After a while, I gently pulled the top of its shell off. The chick was stuck to the shell, but it came loose easily enough.

Only one of the other eggs was moving. Four hatched out of the fourteen I had left, and maybe one more. There were eggs shells all over the incubator. And the chicks wouldn't stop peeping. Kate refused to go to her bed so I let her fall asleep beside the incubator. I lay on my bed and stretched out my legs.

By the time Mom came home I had five chicks. I would have named them, but they kept on moving, and I couldn't tell which was which. Mom carried Kate to bed, and I went to sleep with the sounds of peeping.

* * *

BY THE NEXT DAY THE CHICKS WERE RUNNING, not walking, inside the incubator. I left the unhatched eggs in there, just in case, but I lowered the temperature like the book said to do for the chicks.

"When will the other chicks hatch?" Kate asked.

"I don't know," I answered.

Kate and I laughed as we watched the chicks. Mom watched a bit then went for a shower. My chicks pecked at each other's toes and bits of eggshell.

"They're hungry," Kate said. "Roger, what do baby chicks eat?"

"Seeds," I told her, "but they don't need any yet." I had read that my chicks didn't need food or water for two days.

"What they need is a place to stay." Mom stuck her head into my room on the way to the shower. She smiled at the chicks in spite of her sharp tone. Then she said, more gently, "If the super finds them we could lose our apartment."

Kate looked at me with big eyes. The Building was supposed to be pet-free, although I knew some people snuck in quiet pets, like cats or guinea pigs. Now, new life had hatched inside the Building—inside my apartment. That shouldn't be bad, but it would be to some.

"I know," I said.

"I'm sorry, Roger." Mom's voice softened into a whisper.

She was right. The Building was no place for five grown chickens. Besides, I had nothing to feed them. I could hatch them but I couldn't feed them. I had to find them a home.

* * *

I DIDN'T CARE ABOUT ANYBODY ELSE'S BUSINESS at school that day. Tony could have pinned anything on me and I wouldn't have minded. My chicks had hatched. What else mattered?

Yet when I came home from school, I could hear their wild peeping from the hall.

"That racket is driving me crazy," Mom said as soon as I got into the apartment. "I had to do something with them."

Mom had moved my chicks. The eggs were still in the incubator, along with my five chicks. But the incubator was stuffed into my closet with a long extension cord coming out.

I couldn't keep my chicks in the closet. I had to find them a place. Where? Nothing to feed them. Nowhere for them to live. What could I do?

Just then a knock came at the door. I opened it. Mag Jennings was standing on the faded orange hall carpet in a bright pink winter coat, her arms folded across her chest and a cigarette in her mouth.

Oh no! I thought. Tony told her about the eggs!

I tried to fill the whole doorway with my body.

Mag held her cigarette out between her two fingers. "No pets allowed in the Building," she said with smoky breath.

"I, uh ..."

"And don't tell me you don't have none 'cause I can hear them."

"Who told you?" I asked.

"Ferchristsake, no one told me! Anyone can hear them clear down to the elevator!"

"Oh."

Mag shook her head. Some ashes fell onto the rug. "I've heard of dogs, cats, and hamsters. But never damn chickens!"

"I don't have any place to take them."

"Take them to Middledale Farm, ferchristsake! Just get them out of here. Now."

She walked away, puffing. I held onto the metal doorframe.

Middledale Farm. I hadn't thought of it. Of course a farm would take them.

* * *

MIDDLEDALE FARM WAS A KIND OF PETTING ZOO run by the city. Mom used to take Kate there before the support payments stopped and she started working double shifts at the restaurant.

The guy at the farm looked at me strangely when I walked in. I had an incubator full of chicks peeping and pecking like crazy. He took me to the guy in charge. His name was Frank.

"It's not our policy to take in animals," Frank said. He was bald and his forehead wrinkled when he frowned. "This isn't Animal Services."

"I know. I just thought you could take care of them. My dad kind of dropped them off and I don't have a place for them."

He peered at my chicks.

"Leghorns?"

"What?"

"Are they Leghorns?"

"I don't know what they are. Some kind of chicken, I guess."

Frank laughed. "They're chickens all right. Come on. Bring them over here."

Frank put my chicks in a cage with a light and some

mashed seeds and water. He dipped each chick's beak into the water before he set it down.

"So it can find the water," he explained.

I knew then that Frank would take good care of my chicks.

* * *

EVERY FEW DAYS, I VISITED MY FIVE CHICKS at Middledale Farm. Sometimes I brought Kate. Frank moved my chicks in with the others after a while, but I could tell which ones were mine because they were smaller than the rest.

One day in spring, about two months later, I sat on a wooden chair in the barn, watching all the chickens. The chicks had grown so fast and eaten so much that I couldn't tell them apart anymore.

The chair I sat on was old and the paint had worn off into smooth wood. It was too small for me, and a bit uncomfortable, so after a while I got up to sweep the floor with a straw broom. There was a mother pig grunting to her piglets and a few goats in the barn, too. It reeked way worse than the Building, but in a nicer, cleaner way.

I followed the old tabby cat named Warren outside. The day was warm and sunny, and the snow had melted. A few chickens scratched and pecked at the wet grass while one big rooster bossed them around. Some little kids came and went with their mothers, but I didn't mind them.

Soon Frank came striding up the path in his jean overalls and stood beside me. He was carrying the milking pail.

We leaned on the split-rail fence with his pale elbow and my brown one almost touching. The chickens paraded around in front of us.

Then Frank said, “I’ve seen you sweeping.”

“Yeah,” I answered, not sure if I was about to get in trouble for it.

Frank smiled so I could see his crooked bottom teeth. “Thought maybe you’d want a job helping with the animals.”

He looked back to the chickens. I didn’t know what to say.

“Only part-time, mind you,” he continued. “Not much pay. But it’s good work.” He wiped his dirty hands on his overalls and put out one hand to shake mine. “What do you say?”

I thought about it as the sun warmed my back. Frank grinned wider at me, waiting. Then the rooster crowed loud and strong. The chickens clucked back to him. I smiled, squeezed Frank’s hand, and shook it hard.

“When can I start?”

Leg Fungus

Tanya

Apt. 901

In the school cafeteria, Jennifer and Selene were talking about how to shear the unwanted hair off their legs. There were rows of us sardined onto benches, stuffing food and sharing gab, and they were talking personal.

"Shaving dries out my skin like it's sandpaper," Jennifer said. She was beside me in the aisle seat, stretching her pale legs out sideways like bait. With her long hair dyed black and her skin powdered white, all she needed was a set of fangs to complete the vampire look.

"Oh, girlfriend!" Selene flipped her genetically beautiful blond hair away from her carefully made-up face. She gripped Jennifer's arm with a palsy-walsy squeeze and leaned in as if she were about to reveal her deepest secret. "It burns my skin for days afterward."

My stomach churned. How could they even care about this?

Flynn nodded his head like he understood this crazy talk. Flynn, who had squeezed into our girls' group somehow and made a space for himself. Probably was after Jennifer, since she and Tony were off again, but he didn't stand a chance.

Dad had always said I was too hard on people, but I was hard on myself, too. I didn't exactly get a genetic goldmine when my DNA map was formed. Oversized breasts that got way too much attention. Mouse brown hair that hung limply from my head and plagued my legs, and an abundance of fat cells that multiplied too freely.

"My mom gets her legs waxed." Selene picked up a french fry between two manicured fingers. "She wants me to come too, but you have to let the hair grow long between waxing jobs. Yuck! It looks like the stubble of a man's beard." She nipped off the end of the fry.

Jennifer and Flynn nodded their heads. I munched my beansprout-and-tomato sandwich on organic muesli bread and wondered why leg hair was such a big deal. I shaved mine, but only because it grew in like thick moss on my tree-stump legs. Yet this conversation was beginning to show me just how ridiculous shaving really was. What was the matter with a little leg hair anyway?

"Have you tried that hair remover cream?" asked Jennifer.

"Eww, I did," said Selene with a show of her Colgate teeth. "It burned my skin even worse. What about electrolysis?"

Selene's parents, both big-time real-estate agents, had enough money for anything she wanted. Selene was the only one of us who didn't have to survive the Building. The lucky thing lived in a long stretch bungalow over on Bluegrass Crescent.

"Too expensive," Jennifer dismissed her. "What do you use, Tanya?"

I was going to set into them for even talking about this superficial fluff, but before I could open my mouth Flynn butted his way in.

"My mother plucks the hair on her legs," he said with pride in his voice.

What! Plucks the hair on her legs! I got an image of Flynn's mother, three floors below me in the Building, bending over herself in the bathroom with the door locked tight behind her. Hours of plucking, squeezing eyes shut tight with the pain of pulling out one stubborn hair at a time. Why would anyone want to do that?

Flynn smiled. "My mother is the greatest. She has no more hair growing on her legs. Years of plucking have left her legs smooth."

Flynn noticed his mother's legs? Did he watch her pluck? Too weird. Even worse, he was proud of his mother for torturing her body. I couldn't let it go.

"What is this—an ad for silk stockings?" I muttered under my breath, but loud enough for Flynn to hear me.

"What did you say?" asked Flynn, a plop of mustard on his face. His pale brush-cut hair bristled in defense.

I went for it. "Your mother is sure some kind of saint. Plucking hair by hair, year after year—what a sacrifice!"

Flynn and the others had their mouths hanging open wide like donut holes.

"What I wonder is, why would she do it?" I continued, my voice rising. "Why submit to the pain and boredom of plucking the hair that grows there naturally?" I was on a roll now. "For your Dad? To create herself as the ideal woman? What is the matter with hairy legs anyway?" I was yelling now. "We are animals."

Flynn's mouth flopped open and shut in speechless amazement. Everyone else stared. You would have thought someone turned off the volume, unplugged the speakers. Even people from the next table were listening in, although I guess they couldn't help it.

I wasn't sure how to take all the surprised faces that were turned to me. So I took a bite of my sandwich, chewed slowly with my chin up, and stared at the wall behind Flynn's head. Never again would I shave or even wax, cream, or pluck a hair on my body. No matter how hairy I got. That razor was trash as soon as I got home.

* * *

THREE MONTHS LATER, I'D GROWN A FULL COAT of leg hair. In my bedroom, I liked to admire my legs in my full-length mirror. The hairs on my legs were dark brown—not like the fair ones on my arms. Yet I liked them—dark serpents released from an underground prison. I was whole, balanced, the way I should be. Although I knew that other people wouldn't see it that way.

Luckily, it was winter when I let my hair grow, so no one could discourage me. Iain might have unveiled my legs, even touched them, if we were still together. Yet he couldn't handle me speaking my mind.

Iain and I had been treading water around each other—trying to decide how deep to get. Until he bought an old junker of a car, a real hazard. He had got it for me, he said, so we could be private. When I saw it, I had refused to get in.

"See that black smoke shooting from the exhaust pipe?" I had asked him. "That is death itself." I told him to ditch the car, but he ditched me instead.

Freedom of speech is such a turn-off to some. Leg hair might be an even bigger turn-off.

* * *

I KEPT MY LEG HAIR TO MYSELF. Until, in spring, the freak greenhouse-effect hot weather arrived. Mag Jennings, the Building super, ordered two old guys to clean up the pool a bit and stir in enough chlorine to give us all cancer. Humans are such a curse to nature.

The pool wasn't a total rat-hole. The concrete around it was rough enough to shred a bathing suit, but a cool splash was worth it when my apartment turned into a sauna. Leg hair or not, I started to get the idea of swimming. So did Selene, who called Jennifer one Saturday morning, and Jennifer called me. We all gathered at Jennifer's apartment to get ready.

I knew Jennifer and Selene would probably make a fuss over my leg hair and I tried not to care about what they would think. They would hardly notice. It was a statement for myself. Yeah, sure.

Right away in the musty steam that had been captured by the Building and routed into Jennifer's room, Jennifer and Selene were trying not to stare.

Jennifer was in a simple black bathing suit, of course. Very goth. Selene had the latest two-piece. I was struggling into my too-small floral suit from last year, trying not to fall over as I strained to pull it over my thighs.

"What?" I pretended not to know what they were staring at.

Jennifer ran a hand along my hairy leg and pretended to prick herself on some stubble. I smacked her hand away. She had it all wrong. My leg hair was soft and warm. When I stroked it, it was a fuzzy peach under my hand.

"Did you lose your razor?" asked Jennifer with a vampire's smile—she was showing her fangs. Then she and Selene exploded into the laughter they could hold back no longer.

"Like maybe you should braid it?" said Selene.

"Or tie it with ribbons!" said Jennifer.

The walls of Jennifer's room were plastered with magazine cutouts of beautiful women in stunning black outfits. Perfect women. Sexy women. I began to feel their scornful eyes on me. How could Jennifer stand it?

"OK, enough. It's just a little leg hair," I said, but I was wondering if I should try to get out of swimming. If Jennifer and Selene made fun of me, what would people around the pool do?

We headed to the elevator, with them still laughing. I tried to tell myself that no one would really notice.

* * *

KIDS, TEENS, AND OLD LEERING MEN packed the pool. Sidney was there with her man Clive. I saw Louis with a few friends, and a cute lifeguard up on his perch. Tony shot angry darts at Jennifer. I guess he wasn't over her yet.

I put one leg carefully in front of the other, as if that would hide them from everyone. Then I heard Tony say, "Scope the legs on Tanya!"

I felt my cheeks heat up. I slouched behind Jennifer and Selene, who were collecting admiring looks.

"Her mama was a gorilla," yelled a guy I didn't know, and people laughed with him. Jennifer and Selene laughed, too.

The heat of the day pressed in on me. Where could I hide? Everyone was doing a double-o to get a good look at my leg hair. You would think I had a mucus dewdrop hanging from my nose, or terminal acne. I should have known this would happen. I should never have come swimming.

Then I saw Flynn. To greet the heat, he had shaved the blond hair on his head down to only a thin coat of fuzz. His gray eyes were dusty, dark, and full of shadows. Was he still mad at me for talking about his mother?

I didn't much want him to notice me so I ditched my towel in the patchy grass and raced for the pool.

As I neared the safety of the water, Flynn planted himself in front of me. His red towel hung from his shoulders and down over his skinny body.

He puffed his chest out. The words worked up from deep inside him. He said, "That's a serious skin condition, Tanya. Guess you can't swim in the pool today. The sign says 'No open sores or infections.'" He pointed at the wooden sign by the lifeguard chair.

Of course, my legs are not the shapely sort displayed in every music video ever made. Mine look more like timber—thick, gnarly, and wooden. And the hair did take on the look of black fungus. I could see what he was talking about.

Yet Flynn, with his spindle arms and doughy stomach, couldn't see the whole picture. I was all natural now—the way I was meant to be. If I started worrying about leg hair, what would be next? First, a little exercise to flatten the bulge of my stomach? Then, maybe a cabbage-only diet? Then, a part-time job to save for a breast reduction?

A crowd was gathered around now, hovering back a bit, watching my face. Tears threatened at the corners of my eyes. I could either run away crying or give them a show. So I gathered my courage, flashed my legs in my best Marilyn Monroe strut, and uncorked the natural me.

"What? These little old hairs on my legs? That's just leg fungus. Only mildly contagious."

You would have thought that spores were floating in the wind toward them—spores of the deadly leg fungus. I could even see a B-grade movie in my head—The Attack of the Killer Leg Fungus. Barbie-doll girls running in every direction away from the cloud of spores. Running from the ultimate attack—an attack against the perfection of flawless, hairless skin.

Really, some people did laugh, but most everyone took one giant step away from me—they couldn't even take a joke. I strutted to the pool's edge and tried to dive like an Olympic medal winner since all eyes were on me.

The cool water muffled the voices and the laughter. I swam until I had no more breath then burst to the surface. I squinted over at Flynn in time to see his red face. I had upstaged him—squashed his joke with a better one. He was standing still, embarrassed and angry, as if someone had just pulled down his swimming trunks and left him naked for all to see. I would have to be cautious of him for a long time.

Jennifer surprised me then. "Bag your face, Flynn. It's just a little leg hair."

I couldn't believe it. Jennifer was speaking up for me.

Selene looked sympathetic for a moment, then she said, "Sure looks like some kind of fungus though."

The vampire and the model broke into another giggle fit. I sighed. Flynn scurried over to Tony. The crowd broke up. The show was over. Time to move on to the next victim.

From the water, I glared up at Jennifer and Selene, who were still giggling, and thought about how I desperately wanted to leave. To run up to my apartment and shave my legs with Dad's razor. Because I had enough trouble keeping up with Jennifer and Selene. Because I had enough trouble getting noticed by the guys. I didn't need this. What was the use of making a statement if I had to wear jeans all summer just to hide my legs?

Then I got a vision of myself, balancing on the edge of the tub with the bathroom door locked, just like Flynn's mother. Lathering and then pulling the razor up my leg from ankle to knee with a jerky stroke. The blade wouldn't glide over my skin. It would jump over my stubborn hairs and rip my flesh. I would have to shave twice to do the job right. Swish the hair, blood, and soap down the drain. Bandage the biggest wounds. A punishment for doubting myself.

No. I couldn't give up now. Shaving would mean defeat. It *was* worth it to stand up for what I believed in. I *liked* both my thick brown hairs and my downy blond ones. I would *not* buy into the beauty myth, no matter what anyone said.

Just then, Jennifer and Selene jumped into the water near me. I tried to forget about how they had laughed at my hair and remember how Jennifer had stood up for me.

Jennifer's head bobbed out of the water on one side of me. Selene was on the other.

"Thanks." I half-smiled at Jennifer as she wiped the water from her eyes.

She smiled then raised her hand out flat toward me.

I met Jennifer in a high five.

"Girl power!" Selene yelled.

"I hate when you say that!" I glared at Selene.

Selene shrugged and dove under the water toward the cute lifeguard sitting high up in his chair. Jennifer headed after her. I lay back, took in a deep breath of chlorine and salt, and let the water hold me up. The sky was so blue it stung my eyes.

The Queen of Spades

Jennifer

Apt. 721

I HAD TO LOOK GOOD. Max was in town. One last check in the full-length mirror by the door.

"Why do you always wear black?" Johnny stood behind me in the kitchen with the fridge open, probably hoping that some fully cooked tidbit would miraculously appear. A laugh track exploded from the TV in the living room.

"Because I'm misunderstood."

In his gray sweats and brown plaid shirt, my brother could give me nightmares. I twirled open my favorite lipstick, Ruby Nightshade, and puckered at my reflection.

"What do you mean?" He sniffed a tinfoil package then shoved it back in the fridge.

If only he knew.

"Like in the middle ages, when they burned country women at the stake just because they knew healing herbs."

Dark burgundy lips, glistening wet. So dark they were almost black. Against my white skin the effect was stunning. I ruffled my hair, Mystic Raven #26, and scrunched the long snaky curls into shape.

"What are you talking about?" Johnny scratched his head. The fridge puffed out cool air.

"Black is for the mysterious and misunderstood." I turned sideways and examined my profile in the mirror. A black vinyl dress with fishnets and lace-up boots. My thick waist barely showed. "And it takes off inches. Very slimming."

"You're crazy."

"No, I'm misunderstood." I wrinkled my nose at the rank fridge smell. Cute look. Wrinkled again. Got to use that. I snapped my makeup bag shut and dropped it into my leather bag.

"I'm out of here, baby bro. Stay out of trouble."

"You too."

I slammed the apartment door. Max, here I come.

In the hall, old Berta Streetwater from 710 widened her eyes when she saw me. She wore a matted orange robe with matching slippers and held a plastic bag of garbage in one hand. Curlers in her hair and sloppy salmon lipstick.

Morbid fashion statement. I ignored her. On the way to the elevator, I practiced my catwalk. Shoulders back, chest out, high stepping, hips swaying. I could lure anyone to me—guy or girl. Sizzle.

The elevator dinged. The doors opened. Bill stepped out—he was my mother's latest. Berta stood between us, by the garbage chute.

"Where're you going?" Bill wore a white T-shirt under his dirty spring jacket. His fat hung over his belt. Disgusting.

I flipped my hair over my shoulder and wiggled my hips wider as I passed by Bill and Berta, with her reeking garbage. The elevator doors clanged shut.

"Answer me, girl." Bill grabbed for my arm but I slipped out of his grip.

"Out."

No way I was going to let him get hold of me again. Creep. He'd made a pass at me more times than Tony had.

Nosey Berta dumped her garbage slowly so she wouldn't miss the scene. It clattered down the chute.

"Get back here," Bill bellowed.

Berta snorted, then scurried back toward her apartment. No help from her.

The lights showed the elevator was up on the tenth. I dove down the stairs.

* * *

IN THE LOBBY THE SUPER, Mag Jennings, was scrubbing graffiti off the wall by the elevator. One circular cream spot on the yellowed wall.

"Hey, Mag!" I called as I whizzed by her.

Mag was a tough old broad and I liked her for it. She nodded at me then puffed on the cigarette between her lips. A long ash fell into her pail with a hiss. That woman smoked two packs a day and would brag to anyone how she hadn't got cancer yet. Not much of a role model, until you saw her stand up to a couple of street punks.

The lobby smelled stale. Disgusting. Tanya was waiting for me inside the front doors in faded jeans that showed how wide her hips really were and a lumpy hot-pink sweater. Tony and Flynn were there, too—probably looking for something to do.

"Nice outfit. You wearing that to the club?" I said, trying to give her a gentle fashion hint.

Flynn was checking me out without trying to hide it, but Tony just glared at me. He'd been mad since I'd ditched him a couple months back. I hoped he'd get over it soon. I really had liked him; I just didn't want him. How could I explain?

"And you're going for the skanky look?" Tanya looked me up and down.

You had to love Tanya's mouth. "You know it." I smiled at her and gave her a hug.

"Which club?" Flynn asked.

I decided to test my flirting powers, just to see if I still had it. Tracing one black fingernail down Flynn's cheek and onto his throat like a knife, I said, "You wouldn't be thinking of following us, would you?"

My breasts were about level with his eyes. Flynn gulped, glanced at my breasts then up to my face. He was smiling and his cheeks were scarlet.

Beside Flynn, Tony was shuffling his feet. Out of the corner of my eye, I saw he had that hungry, needy look. God, he still wanted me. You'd think he'd move on.

I looked back to Flynn and lost interest. He was such a scrawny mouse. Tony looked like an Italian thug, but he had a bleeding heart. I couldn't hurt him anymore. I pulled back my hand and adjusted my dress over my breasts.

"Well, you're not coming. Girls' night out. We're meeting Max."

Tony got his mad face on. "Who said we wanted to?"

Flynn's smile fell. "Who?"

I didn't bother to enlighten him. Max was Selene's cousin-by-second-marriage from New York. Her full name was Maxine but I liked her better as Max. She was max, too.

Like last summer, when we'd spent that week at Selene's cottage. It was right after Petra ran away from the Building for a luxurious life on the streets. What was she thinking? Anyway, Selene was up in the cottage getting drinks. Max and I were on the dock, soaking up the sun.

"Could you do my back?" Max had asked.

I'd rubbed the lotion into her creamy mocha skin. She slung her feathery dark hair down over one shoulder and turned to me. With one arm holding her hair to the side, she half-closed her eyes and blew me a kiss. "Thanks, babe." Her lips glistened wet. Did she mean it? I wanted to kiss her for real, but I couldn't. It was Max that stopped me. What would she do? Would she think I was a freak? Maybe I was.

I wouldn't admit it to anyone, but I had realized who I was and what I wanted that day. Tony was nothing. None of the guys I'd been with were anything. I wanted Max. If only she would want me. I wished I could visit her in New York like Selene did. Then maybe I could make something happen. If I had the guts to go for it.

I pulled Tanya to the door. "Let's go."

"I'm coming. Don't yank my arm."

"I told you," I heard Tony say as we left, "she's poison."

No, I'm not, I thought. Not to Max.

* * *

THE LINEUP OUTSIDE THE PURPLE PELICAN was long, but the doorman let us in with a smile—once I promised him a dance.

The Pelican was hot. We walked down the curved staircase to the mingling area and looked out over the sunken dance floor. Guys in casual baggies through to a girl in a corset. A small goth faction yelled over the music to each other. A guy with a green Mohawk was dancing like a windmill. The lights were neon purple tubing so everyone glowed pale and cool.

It was mostly a check-out fest. Voyeurs counting the dance styles on the floor, and heavy breathers deciding which dancers they wished they could take home. Then there were the shy ones, who just stared at each other wondering what to do next.

The tune was an '80s song. Very cheese. The beat pounded through the floor up into my boots. My legs shook with anticipation. I was getting some admiring looks so I was feeling pretty good.

"Where are they?" Tanya's big boobs bumped against my arm. I took a step back. She wasn't my type.

"Who knows?"

I didn't care that I couldn't see Selene or Max anywhere. I wanted to anticipate their arrival.

I watched the dancers. Green Mohawk smacked a girl in the face. She shoved him back hard. He dominoed a few dancers then bounced away, still dancing.

I laughed. That was why I liked the Pelican. No rules.

Then I saw Max. The most beautiful girl ever. She was level with me, across the pit of dancing, writhing bodies. And she was watching me.

I just stared at her. My cheeks heated up and I got tingly and jittery inside. She had this sideways smile just for me. I waved then wished I hadn't. How lame—waving at her!

"There they are!" Tanya finally noticed.

We started toward each other, weaving through the people on the raised platform that circled the dance floor. Selene followed Max, who towered over her and the crowd. Tanya fell behind and I couldn't wait for her.

"Jennifer, you look fabulous!" Max said over the music.

"You too!" I could barely get the words out.

Max hugged me then kissed both my cheeks. Her hair was silky against my skin. Same sleek straight hair as Selene's, only deep brown instead of blond. She'd cut it shorter—it was just down to her shoulders now—and she'd streaked it white near her face.

"We're going to have a great night," she whispered in my ear.

Did she mean that?

Max was wearing a white belly top that showed a portrait of the queen of spades tight across her breasts, cutoff black jean shorts with a studded leather belt, and black-and-white striped leggings. High cheekbones, rich mocha skin, and almond-shaped gray eyes. Gorgeous.

"Like, we had no trouble getting past that doorman!" Selene was looking proud to be the one who had brought Max. Like she owned her. Like Max was hers alone.

"Anything with tits could get past that bulldog," I said.

Max laughed. So did the others.

Selene was thicker than Max, but she knew how to dress, too. Tonight she was wearing a way-short, clinging, blue skirt with a silver top that looked like lingerie.

"You got your eyebrow pierced!" Tanya said to Max after a quick hug. "Does it get infected easily?"

Max raised the eyebrow in a sexy way. "Never, Tanya, baby."

A jealous pang. Max would never go for Tanya, would she? I wanted Max to look at me that way. Like that day on the dock.

A girl with her hair dyed purple to match the club walked by carrying a tray high over her head. She was dressed all in black, with the Purple Pelican logo on her shirt.

"Like, we need some guys to buy us drinks." Selene began to eye a crowd of men near the bar who had already noticed us.

No, I thought. No competition for Max. "Let's just hang together."

"What fun is that?" Tanya said.

"Yeah, we want some excitement, don't we, Max?" Selene elbowed her.

"Sure."

The guys were smiling at us. Selene smoothed her top and stuck out her chest. Tanya slung one hip out and giggled. Max smiled and gave my hand a quick squeeze.

"Just a drink," she said.

I loved how she was trying to take care of me.

The guys left the bar and wandered over. What could I do?

"Wanna dance?" the cutest one asked Max. He had short sandy hair, the stubble of a beard, a strong chin, and a thick neck.

Before Max could answer, Selene grabbed his hand. "Great!" She pulled him down the stairs to the dance floor. Selene's a skunk, but she did me a favor.

Soon we were all dancing. Not that I wanted to. Max got the fat guy, so that was good. Tanya hooked onto the jock. Big and stupid. Probably liked football. I ended up with the thin one. A mirror of black clothes like my own.

Might as well get a drink out of this, I thought.

I fused with my guy in the usual way and moved with him, watching Max as I did. My guy was a good dancer. I could fake liking him for a while. Not that I wanted him, or any guy. Tanya's guy danced like a square block of wood, tipping his heavy body back and forth with no rhythm. Max was laughing at something the fat guy had said. I tried to catch her eye but she didn't notice.

No chance to get close. I had to think. It went this way every time Max came in. Go to a club. Meet some guys. Get drinks out of them. I didn't want this again. How could I make this go my way?

"Let's get a table," I said to my guy.

"Great. I'll buy you a drink," he crooned into my ear.

I smiled and tilted my head toward him—the old habits kicking in. "Red wine."

"I'll have one, too." Selene looked at her man.

"Me too," Tanya and Max said together, then laughed.

We found a tall table we could squeeze around, standing up. The guys disappeared.

"Like, how long do you give them?" Selene giggled.

"Three minutes." Tanya checked her watch.

The faster the drinks came the more desperate the guys were. Sixty-eight seconds was our record. Three and a half minutes later, the guys reappeared with wine and beers. Too slow.

"Cheers, doll," said Tanya's guy. He smashed his heavy beer bottle into her glass, spilling some of her drink. A red stain spread across her pink top.

"I am not a doll," Tanya mouthed off at him. "And don't spill my drink."

Go, Tanya! I managed a laugh and gulped back all my wine.

"You want another?" my guy asked.

"Of course." I sent him off. Now to get to Max.

But Selene's guy had managed to get himself between Max and Selene, and he was chatting up Max. Selene was trying to interrupt, but he blocked her with his shoulder. On Max's other side, the fat guy was trying to get her attention, too.

God, would I ever get close? Suddenly the Pelican didn't look so hot anymore. Peeling black paint. Pipes running across the ceiling. Dried crud on the table. Was this going to be just another lost night?

Tanya and her jock were actually hitting it off. Selene was trying to pull her guy back to the dance floor and away from Max. Max was talking friendly to both the guys who were after her. Then my guy turned up again with my second drink.

"Here you are, babe." He put one arm around me.

He smelled like cheap cologne. I pushed him off. This was turning into a guy-girl pairing. I couldn't stand it. I had to do something.

I pushed past the fat guy and shoved my way into Max's conversation. I met her eyes.

"Want to dance?" I extended my hand, palm up.

The question wasn't so weird at the Pelican, where anything goes. Would Max get my meaning?

There was a beat of silence. I realized that every person gathered around our small table was staring at me.

I shivered. My hand trembled, suddenly cold and exposed. Why didn't Max say something? I continued to stare into her eyes. She didn't break my gaze, but she didn't answer me either.

Then Selene's guy piped up. "What, are you gay, or something?"

Tanya's guy sniggered, like it was some great joke. His shoulders shook with laughter. Max's eyes became more intense. Selene gasped.

"God! Oh, god! No way!" Selene was waving her hands in front of her like she wanted to push me away.

She knew. She knew. Come on, Max. *Say* something.

"What's going on?" my guy asked.

"So she's gay. It's no big deal. I figured it out ages ago." Tanya sounded calm.

Shut up, I wanted to scream. *I don't care what you think*. I only wanted an answer from Max. She had to know what I was asking. What would she do? What was she thinking?

Selene linked arms with Max, her chin sticking out defiantly. I knew what she was saying. That I had no claim. That Max was her cousin, her friend. But it wasn't up to her.

Then finally, Max's face broke. She smiled and the chaos around me melted away. "Love to."

It was that simple. Everyone fell silent. Max shook Selene off and put her hand in mine. We walked that way down the stairs to the dance floor. My hand hot in hers and my whole body singing with pleasure.

The music was blasting in my ears. Some boppy tune—I don't even remember what song it was. I softened into Max, and we grooved like we belonged together. Our eyes were locked, even when Mohawk guy tried to slice between us. The next song was slower. Max smiled, leaned in, and gave me a long kiss on the lips. Her lips were soft, so soft. A cinnamon scent. She lingered just long enough to make me want to dive in for more.

I don't know how long we danced, but after a while I saw Selene and Tanya at the railing watching us. The guys were with them.

Selene looked a bit huffy but now she had three guys fawning over her. Tanya was just enjoying her man. She gave me a thumbs up. "What took you so long?" she mouthed over the music.

I gave her a thumbs up right back and slid closer to Max. This was me—the real me—and I didn't care who saw. Johnny, Flynn, or even Tony.

I'm not misunderstood now, I thought.

I wrinkled my nose in that sexy way and twisted my hips until my black vinyl dress slid against Max's jean shorts. Max smiled and rubbed her queen of spades against me. Delicious.

Take the Stairs

Tony

Apt. 818

My bat smacked the ball with a satisfying crack. I knew it was well hit from the warmth that spread across my shoulders and into my arms. I tossed the bat to the side and began to sprint down the first base line.

"He can hit, too!" the guy named Lorne said, loud enough for me to hear.

I fired the jets a bit more. I could run, when I wanted to.

As I rounded first I eyed the guy in the outfield who was scrambling for the ball. A novice. Didn't even follow the arc. These little rich guys didn't know so much. I predicted the ball would be over the fence.

When the ball went out of the park I slowed my pace, but I slid into home lying down full on my side, just for kicks. The novice was still trying to climb the fence.

A chorus of raunchy cheers rose up, making me smile.

"All right!" Lorne, in his sharp clothes, walked toward me, his shoulders punching the air. He was about my age but he must have had a job to be able to afford those clothes.

"Where'd you come from, anyway? I've never seen you here before." Lorne lifted his shades to get a better look at me.

"Just passing through." I picked myself up. I wasn't going to tell him that I cut through this neighborhood on the way back from my cousin's place just to save the bus fare.

"We smack the ball around here most Sundays," Lorne said. "Maybe you can drop by next week. If you're on my team."

"Sure. Nothing else to do."

"Great." Lorne slapped me on the back and a cloud of dust fell over us. "Need a ride?"

Guys and girls around us were jumping on bikes, heading toward cars, talking over the plays.

"Huh?"

"Do you need a ride, buddy?"

The Building sprang into my mind. The balconies speckled with rust. Broken crap lying all over the place. Crazy Tate who would dash out at a car as it pulled into the circle, just to freak out the driver. Tate was harmless enough, but he had lost too many of his brain cells during the sixties.

I hesitated, thinking up my excuse. I was about to lie that I'd brought my father's car when I saw the girl.

She walked up beside Lorne and linked arms with him. I could see her curves under her shorts and tank top. Too bad she was Lorne's girl.

"Hey, big brother. Let's go."

I let out a breath that I didn't know I'd been holding. Not Lorne's girl. Maybe she'd be interested ... but no. Not a little rich girl.

"Hey, Sue. This is Tony."

Sue's eyes fell on me, and I began to heat up.

"Nice moves." She jerked her chin at me then turned away, distracted.

Her brown hair was tucked under a backward baseball cap but I wanted to see her hair loose. I imagined it falling like a tent over my face—so close the air between us was overpowered by an animal scent. Her long legs wrapped around me.

I shook my head to get rid of her. She was invading me like a virus.

"Hey, bud?" Lorne smacked a ball into his glove.

"Uh?"

Sue was examining her nails as if deciding which one to devour. The curve of her nose was a delicious mini ski jump.

"That ride?"

"Sure."

I followed them toward a Jimmy. Sue got in the front with Lorne. The sun gleamed off the side of the truck so that I had to squint to find the handle, hot to the touch.

I opened the door part way. New-car smell wafted over me as waves of heat poured out.

"Get in." Lorne started the engine.

"Right." I slid into the seat behind Sue. Lorne was blasting the air conditioning and opening all the windows with the remote controls. Sue took off her hat and her hair fell down to her shoulders. She hung a bronzed elbow out her window. I tugged the door shut.

"Where do you live?" Lorne asked, swinging the Jimmy out of the parking lot.

Sue turned the radio to a Psychedelic Furs tune.

"By the valley." The air was whooshing through the Jimmy but sweat still poured out of me.

"Way down there?" he yelled over the music.

"Yeah."

The skin on Sue's shoulders was smooth and tanned. A few long hairs hung over the seat. I stroked them with the back of one finger. Jerked my hand away when Lorne turned to talk baseball. Sue was nothing like Jennifer had ever been. Jennifer had been easy to get, but she stung like hell. Ever since she'd cheated with Josh I told myself she wasn't worth my time. Now I heard she was dating some girl from New York! Unbelievable.

I didn't want Sue to see where I lived, so I had to get Lorne to drop me someplace. Not too far a walk in this heat, though. The ride was nice. Then I thought of Mickey's house, with its three-car garage and a pool. His parents were away for the weekend. Only Mickey and his brother would be around. Mickey's house would be mine today. Perfect.

"You know a guy down there by the name of Valentine?" Lorne asked. "Lives on Sherbet Street?"

I'd heard of him. Played ball with him. Sherbet was three streets from the Building. Mickey's street.

"No," I said.

Sue flicked her hair out of my reach.

"Oh." Lorne sounded disappointed. "He's our second cousin."

Damn. Not Mickey's house then. Maybe I could just get them to drop me at a corner somewhere.

I leaned forward into Sue's zone, pretending to listen to Lorne. She smelled sweet, like I'd expected. My head spun. I backed off.

Then I caught a glimpse of Sue's eyes in the passenger side mirror. Curious and amused. She had seen me lean into her, but she didn't tell me off.

* * *

TEN MINUTES LATER, I WAS STILL TRYING to figure out where to get dropped. The windows were rolled up because the air conditioner was finally cooling. I told Lorne to head down Sherbet Street. Maybe I could make this work out. I would play it loose.

Mickey was in front of his house playing basketball with a few guys. His brother, a guy I didn't know, and Valentine.

Damn.

Lorne pulled the truck to a stop in front of Mickey's. I cracked the window open. Mickey saw me.

"Tony! What are you doing here?"

Good thing I didn't tell Lorne this was my house.

"Just getting a ride." I winked at Mickey after his eyes checked Sue over.

"Hey, Valentine!" Lorne called across Sue in the passenger seat.

Valentine strode over to the Jimmy, his big knees bending sideways like a giant grasshopper's. He was squinting against the sun, trying to peer into the truck.

"Lorne! Sue!" he called when he got up close. Then he saw me. "Hey, Tony!"

Lorne spun to look at me. "I thought you didn't know Valentine."

I shrugged. "Oh. *This* Valentine. I thought you meant a different one."

Like I knew hundreds of guys named Valentine. What guy would want to be named Valentine, anyway?

Lorne shook his head and let it go. He and Valentine got to talking.

I opened my door. "You can just drop me here. I'll walk."

My hand was resting on the back of Sue's seat. I had one foot out of the Jimmy. Sue swiveled and put her hand over mine. Her hair swung out like a fan as she turned and her sweet scent invaded me again.

"No, we'll take you," she said.

My head was probably lolling around on my shoulders as I drooled over her. Sue was way better than Jennifer. I had to get in with her. I wanted her, but I wanted her for keeps.

"Sure," I said to Sue. "You can drive me."

She pulled back her hand. "Great. Which way?"

Valentine and Mickey were leaning in the windows, watching us with needles of jealousy in their eyes. Lorne was ready for directions. My hand was still warm from Sue's. I had to answer her.

I pointed through the front windshield to the Building, which was just peeking over the trees. "Down the street then turn left," I said. "The Monteray. 64 Wilnut Street."

Was I crazy or what? How could I let them drive me to the Building? What was I thinking? Why didn't I just invite them both up to meet my grandfather while I was at it? He used to run a restaurant, so when anyone came to visit he would pile stuffed peppers and cold pizza onto our tiny kitchen table with only two seats and stand over them, calling out, "*Mange!* Eat!"

* * *

THE BUILDING WAS MORE GRAY THAN WHITE, even in the sunlight. Grime was caked onto the walls under the balconies where it had dripped after each rain. Three huge metal garbage bins stood out front, and the stench of rotten food made me close the Jimmy's window.

I hated the Building. I was going to get out of it as soon as I could, but I couldn't pretend I didn't live there. Mickey and Valentine had seen to that.

As we circled the drive, I saw Petra come out of the Building with Magda, a hunched-over Chinese woman who was almost too old to walk, and a younger Chinese woman who must have been Petra's mother because she looked just like her, only scared. Petra and Magda were carrying suitcases over to a small rental van, followed by Petra's mother clutching a thin gray cat. The van was white and pretty beaten up—the kind a million people have used to move their stuff and never cleaned once.

I hadn't seen Petra since she took off in the back of a truck last summer. I'd heard she was living on the streets. Flynn had said he'd seen her downtown once with a hat out for change. If Petra had something to run from, what was she doing back here?

Then Crazy Tate jumped out at the Jimmy. What a maniac! His white hair was sticking up and he was swinging his arms and legs like a lunatic. I figured he was whacked out on something.

"What the …" Lorne began. Sue stiffened.

Crazy Tate tried to climb on the hood of the Jimmy, screaming all the time, but he slid down the driver's side so he just howled into Lorne's surprised face.

"Get off the truck!" Lorne screamed.

Sue laughed. "You live here?"

I laughed too, but for a different reason. Could this get any worse?

Lorne swung his door open and stormed out with his face twisted and his fists ready.

I knew Crazy Tate wouldn't hurt anyone. He only wanted to scare. But Lorne was probably afraid he would scratch his precious Jimmy.

Then, just to add to the confusion, Petra's Dad banged the door of the Building open so hard that I thought it might crack.

"Where do you think you're going?"

He was a tall white guy with a red face and arms as thick as my thighs. Petra and her crew stopped beside the van. He stormed over until he was right in their faces. Petra and Magda put down the suitcases. With the old woman, they moved in a circle around Petra's mother. She whimpered and buried her face in the cat, which was now desperately trying to wiggle free.

"I'll be back in a minute," I said to Sue.

"What are you …"

I didn't wait to hear what she was going to say. I had to get to Petra's father. I knew that kind of look—that kind of guy. The kind that liked to bully people smaller than him. The kind that got power from it. Yet when a guy his own size came up to him, he'd never take them on. At least, that was what I was betting on.

"Hey, Petra! Long time no see. Hiya, Magda," I called out to them as I jogged the space between them and me.

All eyes turned to me. Scared eyes. Mad-dog eyes. Magda took it up first.

"Tony, hey." Her voice was trying to be strong.

I pushed in front of Petra's father and glared into his eyes. His fists tightened. I turned my back to him, hoping he wouldn't hit me. "Petra, can I help you load this stuff?"

Her face was clouded. I think she was wary of me because of that hide and seek game when she disappeared. Maybe we did gang up on her, but it was just a game. I didn't know her father could get like this.

"Sure," Petra said, although she didn't move.

I picked up two suitcases by the handles. The old woman went around to the driver's seat and started the van. Petra and her mother, still shaking, opened the side door and got in—with the squirming cat.

Petra's father looked mad enough to punch in the side of the van. I loaded the rest of the cases then slid the side door shut and tapped it twice.

"You're set," I called.

Out of the corner of my eye, I saw that Lorne had chased Crazy Tate off easily enough. Sue was still in the Jimmy.

I watched the van pull away, feeling the waves of hatred from Petra's father the whole time. I was careful not to get too close to him.

"Now how do *I* get out of this place?" I sighed.

Then Crazy Tate was beside me, bobbing on his toes. "Take the stairs, man." He pointed to the stairs that lead down to the sidewalk and away.

I laughed. "Yeah, right. Easy."

Was it that easy? Could I just leave one day, like Petra had?

I noticed then that Lorne and Sue were watching me with curious eyes. I perked up and walked casually back to them. Helping out Petra was feeling good now—better than a home run. Maybe good things could come out of this Building, sometimes.

"What was that about?" Sue asked.

Lorne was frowning and muttering about Tate.

I leaned in Sue's window, not so ashamed of the Building anymore. Of course, I still hated the paper-thin walls and the puddles in the elevator that smelled like piss, and I still wanted to get out as soon as I could, but I didn't care what Sue saw.

"The usual." I shrugged. "If you liked that, maybe you'd like to come in and meet my grandfather."

What did it matter what I said? The worst had happened. Sue would have to take me as I was, if she wanted me at all.

"What a place you live in!" Lorne shook his head as he crawled back into his seat. "Is everyone this crazy?"

I glanced behind me at the Building. Petra's father was still staring down the street like a rabid pit bull. Crazy Tate bounced around him, but Magda had been smart enough to head inside fast. Then, the sun glinted off a Building window that was covered in tinfoil. The light caught my eye, like a wink, and I got this weird feeling, as if the Building were watching all of us, and listening, too. Like our sounds and smells had seeped into its walls. The good and the bad. The laughs and the sobs. All those scuffmarks and fingerprints, sandwiched between layers of paint. The Building held it all, then let it trickle slowly back to us, like a tribute.

I shook my head to clear it. "Pretty much."

Lorne's hand trembled as he put the Jimmy in gear. I think he wanted to get away from the Building, or at least away from Crazy Tate.

Then Sue said, "So we'll see you at the field next week?"

She covered my hand with hers again, and her fingers brushed back and forth, like a whisper. My temperature soared as her candy-apple smell intoxicated me.

I grinned at her. Lorne may not think much of me now, but he only ever cared that I could play ball. But Sue … she wanted to see me at the game next week. I couldn't believe my luck.

"Wouldn't miss it."

I waved as Lorne peeled out of there. I knew the memory of her would haunt me all week.

Acknowledgements

I AM FORTUNATE TO BE PART of an active and supportive writing community. The Ontario Arts Council generously provided financial support during the writing of this project. Peter Carver, Kathy Stinson, and Barbara Greenwood offered guidance through their writing workshops. The many participants of these workshops provided valuable feedback on the stories as they developed. As writer-in-residence at the University of Toronto, Sarah Ellis commented on an early draft. Margie Wolfe of Second Story Press recognized the value of this project and supported it with great enthusiasm. And Kathryn Cole utilized her considerable talents to make sure every word did its job. Thanks so much to all for your encouragement.

On a personal note, special thanks go to my family. To my children, Paige and Tess, for sharing the fun and the challenges. And to Kevin—my partner in life, work, and play—for the many stories from his Buildings.